It took Fisher's men three days to get Carson back to the Fisher ranch. Carson rode in silence — his stiff, blood-raw hands lashed to the pommel of the saddle, and his feet bound by a rope beneath his horse's belly.

Each day the sun burned down like a blast furnace, forming huge blisters on his neck which burst and ran stinging down his back. His bare feet were shredded past all feeling from walking bootless through the desert, and his tongue was like a swollen, foreign thing puffing out of his mouth.

On the afternoon of the third day one of the men cut him down off his horse. "Fisher may want you alive, Carson, but I want you to travel these last five miles in style. You'll be alive when we get there — but not much else."

Then he took out his knife and rope. . . .

KING FISHER'S ROAD

Shepard Rifkin

PaperJacks LTD.

TORONTO   NEW YORK

▲

PaperJacks

KING FISHER'S ROAD

PaperJacks LTD

· 330 STEELCASE RD. E., MARKHAM, ONT. L3R 2M1
210 FIFTH AVE., NEW YORK, N.Y. 10010

PaperJacks edition published May 1987

ISBN 0-7701-0624-2
Printed in the USA

For Dale and Michael Nortner

Chapter One

Someone had taken an old board and a branding iron and burned in THIS IS KING FISHER'S ROAD TAKE THE OTHER. Then he had nailed it to a fence post. The barbed wire and the fence were also new, but the clay water tank a half-mile down the valley along King Fisher's road was the same one Tom Carson had watered from a year ago. But there was a new barbed wire fence around the tank, as well as a new shanty. The tank was full of water, and Carson's thirty head of cattle, milling behind him, moaned as they smelled the water. They shoved against the wire, heedless of the blood pouring down from the deep gashes. Carson had had to whip them over the heads with his quirt to keep them from turning back ever since sunrise; he was losing control over them, since cattle dying for water go blind.

He reached down from his saddle and opened the gate. The cattle fought to be the first through. Carson's horse butted the ones on the outside in order to force them to make some sort of a regular line. She worked most of the time without any command. Her name was Ten Cents. He called her that because she could stop on the usual dime and give him back nine cents change. She was a three-year-old bay mare and she was the best cow pony Carson had ever had in his thirty-three years of life in West Texas, and in his four years of running his own little ranch. When all the cattle had passed through she halted. A puff of wind passed overhead and the windmill by the pond began creaking. She swivelled her ears forward but remained still, even though she was just as thirsty as the cattle. Carson watched his cattle stumble down the slope. Their two-day struggle across the seventy-five miles of alkali flats and sand had burned fifty pounds off each of them. That meant he would get that much

7

less money for them from the miners at Contention City unless he could find a week's very good grass somewhere.

He pulled one of Ten Cents' ears gently, and when the
last one had gone through he rode down the slope. Last year
there had been a little spring with some cattails. The cattails
were gone and the spring had been enlarged. There was a
barbed-wire fence around that, and a gate with a big new
brass padlock in it. All around the shanty lay rusty tin cans
and empty whisky bottles. There were no horses. Nailed to
the shanty was a small printed notice signed King Fisher.
Again all trespassers were warned, but this time in legal language.

Carson reached in his saddlebag and with a pair of pliers
cut the barbed wire. The cattle shoved through and began
to drink. An old man with his suspenders hanging down
staggered out of the shanty carrying a shotgun.

"Get the hell out!" he shouted. Carson could see the old
man was half-drunk.

"My cattle got to have a drink," Carson said pleasantly.

"You cut the wire, you young son-of-a-bitch!"

"I wouldn'ta cut if I knew you were here," said Carson,
ignoring the insult. He intended to stretch the parley until
the cattle had drunk their fill.

The old man's long tanned face turned red. He moved
closer, holding himself erect by placing a palm against a
fence post. "I got a right to kill you, you whippersnapper!"
he shouted, "cuttin' my wire, comin' onto this yere property.
I tell you, ole King Fisher, he don't give a rebel damn
about your scrawny culls. You git!"

In Carson's left saddlebag was his fortune as far as his
money went—eighty-three silver dollars. "I'll pay you for the
water they drink," he said, and he reached for the saddlebag.
The old man brought up the muzzle sharply till it pointed at
Tom's belly. It wavered a bit, but always within its drunken
oscillation was either Carson's groin or belly or chest. Carson
knew the old man was allowing for his drunken condition
in case he decided to fire.

"Keep yore hands on the pommel, boy," the old man
said softly. He moved a bit closer. Now Carson could see
the tiny broken blood vessels in the old man's narrowed
eyes. His stomach felt ice-cold. A drop of sweat slid down
across it and it, too, felt icy.

"I got money in my saddlebag," he said. "You just take

out ten dollars, an' I'll keep my hands on the pommel."

The old man moved along the fence, touching an occasional post to keep himself erect. "I don't want your cattle piss in my water," he said. "I don't want your goddam money, either. King Fisher'll take my head off when he sees them hoof marks and that cut wire!"

"Twenty."

"Don't turn yore hoss, son," said the old man. Now he was ten feet away. Carson knew the old man intended to get in back of him.

"Twenty-five."

"King Fisher's my nephew, boy. He'll be down on me like the whole Missouri on a sandbar. I'm nothin' but a pore ol' weak man, old enough to be your granddaddy, and you want me to catch hell? He'll eat me raw, without salt, for not shootin' you. You trespassed, you destroyed his property, an' now you're tryin' to offer me a bribe? That's enough talkin'. I ain't runnin' for gov'ner. Now git off yore hoss."

"I'll pay you for the wire I cut. But my cattle had to have water."

"I'm done talkin', son," the old man said heavily. The two barrels jerked a bit as the old man cocked the shotgun. At the dry, ominous sound, Ten Cents' ears pricked sidewards.

"If you're thinkin' of usin' that thing," said Carson, speaking casually and slowly, "you'll hang."

"You damn fool!" chortled the old man. "Sheriff's ol' King Fisher's brother-in-law. King Fisher *owns* Clark County, cows, fences, jails, gen'ral store, and cemetery! Git down. My side."

The old man moved along the fence. His suspenders caught in the barbed wire. He looked down in order to free them and Carson threw himself off Ten Cents, pulling his Colt. He fired from his knees. The old man went down with a blue hole in his forehead as he squeezed both triggers. The double blast tore off Ten Cents' left foreleg at the knee. She screamed in agony and Carson put his second shot through her head. Then he vomited, trembling. The old man's suspenders had caught even more thoroughly in the wire as he fell, so that his skinny behind was uppermost, his tobacco-stained mouth pressed into the dust. The bloodshot eyes glared blindly, as if furious at the dirt of Texas. Several of the cattle lifted their heads and stared, the water dripping off their muzzles. They began drinking again.

The mountains were twenty-five miles away. From what Carson had heard about King Fisher, he knew that the man believed in direct action. Carson's brand was registered in the county seat, and it was burned on every single cow drinking in the pond.

"Goddammit!" said Carson. "I might as well have taken a full page ad in the El Paso paper sayin' I did it."

He had paid eighty dollars for his saddle in Phoenix. He would have to leave it as well as his Winchester. He had some hard-tack, some beans, some coffee. If there had been a horse around he would have taken it and left what he thought it was worth: self-defense was all right, the way he had been brought up, horse-stealing was not. He shot the best steer and cut off several steaks. He would work south along the ridges in the mountains until he came to Mexico, a hundred and seventy miles south, and he didn't want to attract attention by shooting game. He would have to stay out of sight of everyone—the occasional miner loning it up there, the small rancher. He dare not try to buy a horse until he was pretty close to the border.

And the little spread he had saved every cent for seven years to buy—that he could forget about. He would have to walk in his stocking feet to the mountains, his high-heeled boots would raise blisters before he could walk two miles.

He slung the saddlebag over his shoulder and took his last look at Ten Cents. The night before, as he lay trying to sleep she had come to smell him as he lay under his slicker, to see if everything was all right, and then she had gone back to graze. At four o'clock she lay down and slept an hour. He heard her snore and he remembered smiling at that before he had fallen asleep.

"Well, so long, you old flea-bag," he said, and to his surprise he found himself crying. He began walking toward the mountains. He reached them at nightfall, his feet blistered and bleeding. He kept going until he could not stand up any more. At sunrise he got up again, and walked up a dry stream bed, moving from flat stone to flat stone. At nine he stopped and ate some hard-tack and drank some water out of his canteen. He didn't dare to light a fire until he came across some buffalo chips, or some other fuel which would not make any smoke. Far below, across the grass-lands, just about where the windmill would be, he saw a big dust. He screwed the cap on the canteen and ran for his life.

Chapter Two

He spent the night in a little hollow at the crest of a hill. It was cold and he had no blanket. Every pound extra would slow him down. The hill was covered with loose pebbles and stones. Maybe an Apache might come up during the night without a small noisy landslide, but nobody else could. His feet were blistered worse than ever and full of small swollen reddened areas where he had picked up thorns. At the foot of the hill was a narrow reed-bordered creek.

At sunrise he got up, ate some hard-tack, and lifted his canteen for a drink. It was empty. He slowly raised his head behind a clump of mesquite clustered on the rim. In the middle of the creek an Apache, wearing a necklace of polished mussel-shells, sat a horse. The water came up to the horse's belly, and as the horse drank the Apache idly swung his free foot back and forth, splashing the water, and yawning and stretching as he watched the other members of the war party washing and drinking in the creek. Another Apache, sitting his horse nearby, noticed a broken reed where Carson had knelt the night before.

He dismounted, and parting the reeds in front of him with his long lance, began to follow the trail made by Carson through the reeds. The other Apache called to him, irritated, and turned to leave with the others, who were now ready. But the Apache kept on crawling through the reeds. Then Carson saw him suddenly stop. A big female rattler had come out, rattling a few feet in front of him. As Carson watched, she coiled and rattled again. Several baby rattlers were sprawled near her. The Apache withdrew quickly, falling backwards into the creek. His friend asked a question and then laughed. Then they all rode south.

After fifteen minutes Carson went down, giving a big

11

berth to the rattlers. He filled his canteen and moved south, saying "Thanks, mama," to the big rattler, even though he couldn't see her. As soon as he could, he moved to the other side of the ridge, and at noon he saw some crude timber-work half-way up a pine-covered slope. It was a mine opening, and next to it was a small corral with a horse and a mule in it, and beyond that a small shanty. The door was open. When Carson came to the door he saw a dirty miner in a checked woolen shirt frying bacon. His back was to the door.

"Don't turn around and don't drop the pan or I'll have to kill you," Carson said. "Just set the pan on the stove, unbuckle your gun and let it drop on the floor." The man did as he was told. "Now kick it backwards to me."

Carson shoved the gun in his belt. "Where's your rifle?" he asked. "No rifle," the man said grumpily. "Got a carbine."

"All right," Carson said patiently, "where is it?"

The man pointed backwards, still not turning around. The carbine lay across the horns of a deerhead nailed above the door. Carson pulled it down and put it under his arm.

"Whadda you want?"

"I'm buyin' your horse," Carson said.

"You gotta stick a gun in my back to buy a horse?"

"Shows I'm serious," Carson said. "How much?"

"I don't wanna sell her."

Carson said evenly and quietly, "How much?"

"In that case," said the miner, "seventy-five."

"The son-of-a-bitch is so sway-backed he'll drag my feet on the ground. Forty."

"Look here, mister, I ain't bargainin'. You want that horse, he'll cost you seventy-five."

"How much for a saddle?"

"I got a Mex saddle on the bobbed wire back of the shanty. That saddle set me back eighty-five when I was ranchin'.' "

"You used it a lot. And you used that horse a lot. I'll give you eighty-three for the both of 'em. And with a saddle blanket thrown in."

"Nope."

"Eighty-three is all I got," said Carson. He cocked the Colt.

"It's a deal," said the miner.

Carson emptied his saddlebag onto the floor. Then he put back his hard-tack, his coffee, and the steaks. He said, "Saw some Apaches this mornin'. I'll leave your carbine an' Colt a couple miles south. Don't want to leave 'em here. You might get feelin' too cocky as soon as I leave."

"Thanks, but that's no news 'bout Apaches. Them buggers go up and down that valley stealin' horses and sellin' em in Mexico, and stealin' em in Mexico and sellin' em back up here. I leave them alone, they leave me alone. In trouble with Mr. King Fisher?" the miner asked, staring at his badly-chinked wall.

"Now what makes you think that?" Carson asked, picking up a pair of boots and discarding them as too small.

"No offense meant, but that's a foolish question," was the sour response. "Yo're headin' for Mexico like a sick cat takes to a hot brick. Might as well save yourself the trouble."

"What's this King Fisher like?"

"Well, he ain't bad 'cept when he's drunk, and he gets drunk often and stays drunk long. And when he's sober he's just as mean, and he's sober whenever he ain't drunk. When he's sober he just lies there and waits for you to walk by. Like a rattler, but he ain't a gentleman, because he don't rattle. Son-of-a-bitch, that must be the chink where the wind come in last winter and gimme such a crick in the back of my neck. I hadda get some liniment and tear up my old red flannel skivvies—"

"All right," said Carson. "You can turn around. I'm sorry for your aches and pains."

"Thanks," said the miner. He turned around and looked at Carson's feet. He whistled.

"Had a run-in with Mr. King Fisher once," he said. "I had a little spread out by the Rio San Miguel. He was just beginnin' to feel his oats, his cows were always havin' twins or triplets while mine and my neighbors' cows were all barren. He hadn't put up his bobbed wire yet, so my cows would hang around King Fishers' corrals, full of envy for his cows' children, and bawlin' because they had none. I talked it over with three other small ranchers like me, out along the San Miguel, and we were obliged to call around thataway and we threatened to hang him if his cows had any more twins. And you see the result of that little talk? I'm runnin' this shaft alone."

"What happened?"

"Lemme give you some iodine, son. You can take it with you. Out of them four ranchers, I'm the only one alive today. And he got all the property. I had a son, too. He died, full of Apache arrers. It was King Fisher's nephew, Bearclaw Hanson, who found him. I went where Bearclaw said he found him. All the horse tracks around was made with iron shoes. I found a couple cigarette butts around, too. I found boot marks, no moccasin tracks anywheres. I'm alive because I'm yaller—he made me an offer and I sold out. The others died, one in Dodge City, accidental in his hotel room. He was lookin' up the barrel of his Colt and it went off. King Fisher was in the next room, an' he testified at the inquest. Then the other ones, one died of a broken neck, he ran against a low branch in the dark ridin' home; he went by a saloon where some of King Fisher's men used to drink. They found him under a tree with his horse grazin' nearby. They brought him to the sheriff. Bearclaw said it was death by misadventure. His daughter lived back east, and King Fisher made her an offer. It was mighty low, but no one else dared make a bid, so she sold it to him. So let me give you advice, son. I don't know what you did that makes you take off in your stockin' feet, maybe you spit on the floor of the saloon and not in the spittoon, maybe you done nothin' worse than raid a watermelon patch —but you better change yore name right away. An' don't stop when you get over the border and start lookin' for work in one of those spik ranchos—keep goin' till you get south of Durango."

"So long," said Carson. He threw the saddlebag over his shoulder.

"Enjoyed yore visit," said the miner. "Don't get a chance to talk much. If you'd like to set awhile I'll make you some bacon and beans."

"Got to get movin'. Thanks anyway."

"Just put my artillery anywhere you want. Only don't leave them in the sun. Shore would hate to burn my hands on 'em."

Carson slung the heavy, ornate saddle over the saddle blanket. "No trouble to make a mite extra," said the miner. "I make biscuits that would make you slap yore grandmaw."

Carson shook his head and rode away. The little horse was out of condition and resented being forced, and without spurs Carson found him unheeding at being raked with his heels. He tried to graze wherever there was grass, and long before Carson reached a shady place to set down the miners' artillery, he had cracked open his mount's mouth with his irritated jerking on the bit.

It took two hours for the horse to learn that his rider was even more stubborn than he was. He then settled down to a steady pace, and Carson pushed him until it was too dark to see.

Chapter Three

Four days later and fifty miles into Sonora, Carson woke up to a scuffed boot toe prodding him in the back. His hand shot under the saddle he was using for a pillow but his Colt was gone.

Standing around him were four men. The one who had prodded him awake had now come in front of him. He was tall and fat and wore a sheriff's star. His stomach bulged over his gun belt and he stank of sweat, as did the other three.

"S'pose he's the one?" asked the sheriff.

One of the men squatted on his heels, still pointing his Colt at Carson's head. He shoved the gun in the holster and, unbuttoning his grey flannel shirt, pulled out a piece of paper. It was a long telegram, and Carson could read the signature. It said, "Beg to remain, respectfully yours, J. Rodman, County Clerk, Estancia, Texas."

"Lessee, now," said the man. "In re—in response to your telegram of fifth inst'—what the hell's 'inst'?"

"Jesus," said the sheriff heavily, "gimme."

The man handed the telegram to the sheriff. He read rapidly and easily, looking at Carson from time to time, " 'Thomas Carson, owner of Stirrup Bar brand, registered two years ago, as well as I can remember, age about thirty-five, about five-feet-ten, black hair, blue eyes, scar across back of left hand'—"

The man who had squatted let out a triumphant rebel yell. "That's him!"

The sheriff folded the telegram carefully and replaced it in the man's pocket.

"All right," he said, "I arrest you for the murder of Jason Weatherby. Get on your horse."

"You can't arrest me in Mexico," said Carson, knowing he was not being realistic. He was very careful not to make

16

any sudden moves. Two of the men saddled the horse he had bought from the miner while the third went through his saddlebag; not finding any money he turned it upside down. Then he kicked through the contents in disgust. "Nothin'," he said.

"Strip," said the sheriff. Carson got up and stripped, tossing each article of clothing to the sheriff as he did so. He did not wear a money belt and the pockets were empty. "Broke," said the sheriff.

"Damn," said the squatting man, and stood erect, stretching.

"All right, dress," said the sheriff.

They tied his hands to the pommel and his ankles were tied together by a short line running under his horse's belly. "You're lucky," said Bearclaw. "If I had my way I'd leave you to a couple of Apaches. Let 'em spread-eagle down on the flats and let them women work you over. And what are we gonna do?" he said, disgusted. "Set you on a hoss under a cottonwood branch, and slap 'im in the ass. Less'n a minute is all it takes. You're lucky King Fisher is civilized. Shall we mosey on, gennelmen?"

For the three days it took them to get back, Carson said not a word. He couldn't bribe them with money or promises of money—they knew he was broke. Nor, riding with a sheriff, could he claim protection from any of the sheriffs in the hot little cow towns through which he rode bareheaded, while the kids ran alongside yelling, "What's he done, mister?"

Huge blisters formed at the back of his neck. The sun seemed to grow bigger at noonday till the whole sky burned like a blast furnace. They deliberately gave him very little water; it was a blessing in a way, because all he could think about was filling his mouth with water, and his ultimate execution meant less and less to him. Bearclaw wore very elaborate Mexican spurs, and their jingle reminded Carson of sleighbells after the first snow. And that, in turn, made him even thirstier than ever. He began to hate those spurs even more than his captors' attempt to tease him by deliberately spilling water from their canteens as they drank. That he handled by closing his eyes. Once Bearclaw hurled some water in his face while his eyes were closed. Startled, Carson opened them and licked the few drops that remained on his lips. He worked out a fantasy of revenge: he would melt Bearclaw's spurs and wait till Bearclaw begged for water. Then he would take the molten silver and pour it into Bearclaw's eager, gaping mouth. He would first peg him out next to a cold, mountain brook so Bearclaw could hear the icy water rushing over the flat stones at the bottom and could look at the curious trout staring at him through the clear water with their mouths opening and closing, drinking the endless flow from the snow ranges of the distant Rockies.

The last morning Bearclaw lit five fires in a row and threw damp weeds on them. Five columns of thick grey smoke rose in the still air. Carson knew it meant that although four men had gone out, five were coming back. "King Fisher's gonna get some real estate ready for you," he said. "You're sort of gonna be a permanent trespasser, and it ain't gonna cost you a cent."

When Carson saw King Fisher's sign again it was mid-afternoon, and his face was burned raw under a week's growth of reddish beard. One of the big blisters on the back of his neck had broken. His bare feet were blistered and raw, and puffy wherever thorns or cactus spines had dug themselves under the skin. His tongue had swollen. The windmill was motionless. On the fence around the waterhole sat several buzzards, their wings half-opened for ventilation in the still, hot air. The fence had been repaired where Carson had cut it. The buzzards sidled slightly as the men rode by, their snake-like necks twisting to watch. Back of the shanty was the rib-cage of a horse, picked clean by the bulging buzzards. Carson turned his face away.

"I asked could I kill you when I caught up with you," said Bearclaw. "King Fisher said no. Said he wanted everything legal. Said he wanted to see you. Alive." He opened his jackknife and leaned over. He cut the rope holding Carson's ankles together; then he untied his hands from the pommel, handcuffed them, and shoved. Carson went over and landed in the dust on his blistered face. He made no sound.

"Git up," said Bearclaw.

Carson got to his knees and then to his feet.

"He'll get you alive but not much else," said Bearclaw. "We're gonna cover the last five miles in style. You ain't gonna like me for that." He shook out twenty feet of his riata and tied an end to the handcuffs. Then he headed for the ranchhouse at a fast walk. After fifteen feet Carson stumbled over some low brush. Bearclaw pulled him erect

and started again. After dragging Carson several times he
regretfully slowed his pace. After forty-five minutes of this
Carson felt nothing in his feet, which seemed like two large
overstuffed pillows, filled with feathers. They were inefficient
for walking or for supporting him, and they seemed to be
susceptible to rips and tears. They could, however, hold
him up for a few yards at a time if he were not too slow.

He heard one of the men say, "He looks like an ol' sun-
dried bucket about to fall to pieces," and someone answered,
"He don't stand no more show than a stump-tailed bull in
flytime."

Carson was panting like a dog. His tongue felt bigger than
ever as he stumbled and floundered through the ocean of
chaparral covered with grey dust.

The little group trotted to the top of a hill and halted.
Below them lay King Fisher's ranchhouse. It was an adobe
fortress, built around a huge patio in which there were several live oaks and two old cottonwoods. High up, at five-
foot intervals, around the upper rim, were rifle slits. At the
corner closest to the little river that flowed through the bottom of the valley, rose a watch-tower forty feet tall; and just
under its top were the usual rifle slits. Several saddled horses
were grazing among the twisted and trampled sunflowers that
filled the space between the house and the river. From the
crests of the hills surrounding the valley, green meadows
ran clear down to the river, forming a lush, well-watered,
green saucer. Halfway down the hill on which they stood
was a little cemetery. A freshly filled grave lay at one end.
Next to it was one that had just been opened a few hours
ago, as Carson could tell by the still damp root fibers that
lay exposed in the freshly turned soil.

Bearclaw said, "They got my smoke all right." He reined
in. Carson's breath was coming in great heaving gasps that
whistled as his chest labored. The salt sweat running into his
eyes made them smart. He lifted his handcuffed and swollen
wrists to wipe them, and Bearclaw jerked his rope. Carson
fell headlong.

"That grave looks a bit small, don't it, Mr. Carson?" Bearclaw asked. "But you won't mind my doublin' you up, I'm
sure."

"You'd have enough guts for that," said Carson. It was
the first time he had spoken for three days, and his tongue
felt a stranger in his mouth. Bearclaw flushed and the others

tittered. He was jerked viciously to his feet. As he went by
the other end of the cemetery he saw that most of the
markers were plain wooden slabs. Almost all were cowpunchers who had been killed by Apaches or by gunshot
wounds or by a horse. One wooden marker, a little more
elaborate than the rest, said:

JULIA MORGAN FISHER 1849-1875.

Next to it was a tall marble shaft that said:

ANDREW HASKELL FISHER 1871-1875
Children are an heritage of the Lord

Bearclaw spurred his horse to a fast trot. As Carson was
dragged and jerked for the last five hundred yards one savage
thought burned: he had to get his hands on a gun. He
could handle one with the handcuffs on. The only thing
he was afraid of was that Bearclaw has rammed the cuffs
on so tightly that his numbed fingers might not have accurate control of the gun. That was a risk he would have
to take.

Chapter Four

While Carson became used to the dim light inside the house he heard a slow creaking sound. The sound came from a long cylindrical mass that moved back and forth. Several parallel bars of light got their shape from the rifle slits high up in the walls. The hard oak floor felt cool to his bloody soles.

When his eyes adjusted to the light he saw that the dark mass swinging slowly back and forth was a Yucatan hammock. It was suspended from two of the several oak beams that held up the high transverse roof beams. From a nail driven into one of the vertical beams hung a gun belt with a .45 in it. By the deference shown toward the hammock by the men in the huge dim room, Carson knew that King Fisher was in it. As he watched, a spurred boot came out of the hammock and kicked at the floor. The hammock began its creaking but in a quicker frequency. The boot stayed out of the hammock, balanced lightly on the rowel, which rolled back and forth as the hammock swung. By the old, deep scratches in the floor Carson could tell that this was an old habit.

A calm, deep voice growled something. Bearclaw promptly dug out a match and lit the long Havana that King Fisher was holding to his mouth. His hand was big and brown, and a plain, wide gold wedding ring was on the ring finger. The little finger next to it had been blasted off in a gun fight. A cloud of smoke drifted upwards and King Fisher clasped his hands behind his neck and stared at Carson. He was clean-shaven and had big shoulders. Carson figured he was in his early forties. He wore a clean white shirt buttoned carefully to the top, which was held with a little gold stud on which was engraved a tiny rose. His face was in shadow.

Carson looked elsewhere. The room was a hundred feet long and twenty-five feet wide. Several couches covered with buffalo robes lay along the walls. Men were sprawled on them staring at him. Navajo blankets lay three deep on the floor. There were eight tranverse roof beams, hand-hewn a thousand years ago; King Fisher had taken them out of the cave dwellings in the upper Navajo country five hundred miles to the north and had freighted them south when he built the ranchhouse. From each roof beam hung a bronze lamp. Each one held a gallon of kerosene. On each side of the massive oak door was a carbine rack. Each rack held fifteen Winchesters.

"Had a good look?" asked Bearclaw. "Ja get a good look at the wagons outside?"

Carson looked at the ladder going up to the tower. There was a floor high up in the tower, and rifle slits. By craning his neck he could see boxes of ammunition neatly stacked beside each slit. He lowered his gaze. In one corner were sacks of potatoes, dried beans, onions, dried beef, and what looked like barrels of water. And kegs of bourbon. The place was a fortress, built to withstand a long siege.

Carson had seen the wagons. He knew what they were for: to hang him. Two wagons had been lashed together by their front wheels to keep them from separating. The wagon tongues were pointing straight upwards and tied together. They were used to hang men when there was no tree available. But there was a big cottonwood outside in the patio. It had a good, strong horizontal branch fourteen feet from the ground. It was ideal for a hanging, and Carson wondered why they had run the two wagons together. And at that moment, behind him, he heard two men whispering. One said, "How come he ain't usin' that puffectly good cottonwood?"

"Evva since Cousin King Fisher's boy he died," whispered the other man, "King Fisher don't use that tree none."

"How come? Don't make sense."

"That there branch is where the boy used to hang his swing on."

"Ah!" said the other man, respectfully.

"Last time we hung someone," said Bearclaw, "we let 'im hang there for a week. Went by three days later. Coulda swore the man's neck was three feet long. You—"

King Fisher's hand went up slightly, palm outward. Bearclaw stopped talking as if the big square palm had been clapped over his mouth.

"Whyja kill the old man?" King Fisher asked. The voice was soft and pleasant.

"I asked him for water for my cattle. He wouldn't give me or sell me any. He got madder and madder and he pulled down on me with that shotgun an' he was a mite slower than I was."

"Don't give us any of that horseshit!" said Bearclaw.

"All right," said Carson. "You wanna know the real reason I shot him? He smelled bad."

A low amused rumble came from the hammock. It shook a little and subsided. The other boot swung into view and King Fisher sat up, stretching the hammock till it provided a back rest for his big shoulders.

"And dumb!" said King Fisher. "A man with a double-barrelled shotgun lettin' hisself get kilt by a lil ole Colt? That's shameful. I'm shore ashamed to be kin." He blew some smoke at the ceiling. "Dumb!" he repeated with vehemence, slapping his thigh. "Take off his handcuffs. Someone give 'im some water."

Bearclaw reluctantly dug out a key from a pocket. The flesh had puffed out so much around the iron that he had trouble inserting the key. No one made a move to give Carson water. The fingers were theoretically his, Carson knew, but they hung limply, like a bunch of small bananas. Near him slouched a lean youngster on a buffalo-robe covered couch. He had been one of Carson's captors. They called him Archie. His feet were thrust out in front of him. One spur rested on the floor, and the other boot heel was locked into the instep of the other boot. He was making a horrible tuneless whistling. His sombrero was pushed down till its tip rested on his nose.

"Archie!" King Fisher said sharply.

Archie got up angrily and dipped a tin cup into a huge clay olla hanging from a hook. Carson's legs were trembling from the drag through the mesquite and he was forcing them to remain rigid less anyone think he was losing control of himself. Bearclaw was standing three feet away with his thumbs hooked into his gun belt. A level bar of sunlight cut across his bulging belly. For the first time Carson noticed that the butt of the .45 hanging from the nail was made of ebony. Spades, hearts, diamonds and clubs had been cut out of silver and inlaid in the butt.

Archie walked over with the cup of water. Carson knew that Archie would have preferred to throw it in his face, and even though it hurt his raw, burned face, he grinned as he took the cup. He needed both hands to hold it and with great difficulty his fingers obeyed his wish to close around it.

"Think you're the king bee, doncha?" said Archie. He looked down at Carson's feet. "Yuh like the little walk we took?"

Carson took several sips first. "Woulda enjoyed it more if you was prettier," he said critically.

King Fisher roared and slapped his boot. "All right," he said. "Archie, sit down. You asked for it an' you got it." He took a deep inhale and blew the smoke gently upwards. The fragrant blue smoke drifted among the festoons of dried red chile peppers hanging from the ceiling. Carson watched the smoke wrinkle in and around the peppers as Archie, muttering, settled himself on his robes.

"I'd hate like hell to be shut up with you in a winter line camp off somewheres," said King Fisher, staring at Archie. "I shore would." He turned in the hammock. "All right, Mr. Carson, you wanted my water bad, and now you're gonna pay for it. We're gonna have a jury trial first. Don't look so surprised. I respect the law. Get the good Book, Archie."

Archie untwisted his scuffed boots and sullenly picked up a small Bible from an old Spanish cabinet that stood in a dark corner.

"First thing we gotta do," said King Fisher, "is swear in a jury. Swear in a jury, Sheriff." Bearclaw counted the men in the room. There were eight. He stepped outside and brought in four of the men who had been squatting outside. They took off their hats. They were not kin. An old white-haired man began swearing them in.

"I don't think this is gonna be legal," Carson said.

The old man stopped and stared at him. He said savagely, "You believe in the Bible, stranger?"

"Sure. But that's not what——"

The old man stopped and stared at him. He said, savagely, "I'll thank ye not to mock the work of the Lord." He went on swearing the men. Archie did not take his hat off. He lay sprawled on his back, shoving cartridges from a box into his gun belt. When the old man turned to swear him in he had dumped out the shells from his Colt into his hand and was wiping them one by one on his dungarees. The old man held out the Bible. Archie yawned, shifted the Colt to his left hand and placed his right on the Bible. The old man jerked the book away.

"Young whippersnapper!" he said. "You put away that godless piece of junk an' stand up and take yore hat off like a God-fearin' man else I ain't gonna swear you in!"

"Don' wanna be swore in," muttered Archie. "Whyn't we just hoist 'im now? I mean, why we gotta fool around?"

"You get yoreself swore in, Archie," said King Fisher. "We owe our guest a little courtesy. Now you just put away your toy an' stand up like a good boy and do what your uncle Asa says. You hear me, boy?"

"I was wipin' the oil offa mah ca'tridges," mumbled Archie.

"Uncle Asa been here since the year one, only the mountains been here longer. When he tells you to do somthin' you do it."

"Put too much oil on my ca'tridges," Archie mumbled, aggrieved, but he did as he was told. Uncle Asa swore him in. When he had finished, King Fisher turned to Carson and spoke. "Jury swore in. You want a defense attorney? Pick anyone. Pick me, if you want. Pick Uncle Asa, only I gotta warn you, you shot his brother. But if I say he's gonna be yore lawyer, he's gonna be yore lawyer."

Carson wanted to play for time until he could use his hand again. He was equidistant between Archie's gun and the gun belt hanging on the nail. But there would be little point grabbing a gun which he could not hold. He flexed his fingers as unobtrusively as possible, and said, "I want this trial held in the county seat."

The expected burst of harsh laughter came. King Fisher lay back in his hammock and kicked off again, smoking, and grinning as the hammock began its oscillation.

"Now," he said lazily, "that would just inconvenience everyone mighty bad. What with round-up time just about here. An' if we did get enough jurors, why, they'd still be kin, or sort of dependent on my good will, so you wouldn't get a fair trial. Or you'd get some people with mighty unpleasant things said about them—like people sayin' they'd brand anythin' with a hide from a tambourine to a buffalo. An' when men like *that* sit on a jury, they lean over backwards to show how much *they* disapprove of other citizens goin' around cuttin' bobwire and shootin' helpless ol' men. Why, how could you 'spect justice from those? And then they'd hang you under painful circumstances, bein' without experience. So we'll save time and we'll save the county the expense of a trial. Because these gennelmen here ain't expectin' to be paid for jury duty. They wanna save the county money. So who you want for yore lawyer?"

"Lookin' around here at the legal talent," said Carson, "I'll be my own lawyer, thank you kindly."

King Fisher grinned. "All right, Bearclaw," he said. "What's yore evidence that Mr. Carson here trespassed?"

"His cattle was down by the pond."

"You know how to read?" King Fisher asked.

"Yep," said Carson.

"You see that sign on the road?"

"Yep."

"What's it say?"

" 'This is King Fisher's Road. Take the other,' " Carson said.

"You opened the gate anyway?"

"Yep."

"All right. Bearclaw, what's yore proof he cut the wire and destroyed my property?"

Bearclaw held up the pair of pliers he had taken from Carson's saddlebag.

"Place it on the table and mark it 'Exhibit A.' "

"Huh?"

"Nemmind, Bearclaw, I made a joke. You gimme them." Bearclaw tossed the pliers and King Fisher caught them easily with one hand. He toyed with them as he spoke. "You wanna deny anythin' just said?"

"No."

King Fisher's eyebrows lifted. He had expected more fight, as his expression showed. He shrugged, disappointed. "All right, then. Bearclaw, what's yore evidence on the murder charge?"

Bearclaw silently placed a dirty forefinger in the center of his forehead. "Big blue hole," he said. "Smack in the middle."

"In the middle?"

"Dead center."

King Fisher's eyes roamed over Carson. The sensation was slowly coming back to his fingers. They felt as if several very sharp little knives were being twisted around each bone as they spiralled down toward each fingertip.

"You handy with a .45?"

Carson shrugged.

"You got no record. Checked up. You ain't big enough to get yore picture took. You musta run out of whisky bottles to shoot at."

"He swung a double-barrelled shotgun on me."

King Fisher looked at Bearclaw, who said, "No shotgun."

"Yo're lyin' to me, boy," King Fisher said, staring at Carson. His expression was a blend of hard anger and suppressed amusement.

"Then what the hell blew the leg off my horse?"

"What horse?" asked Bearclaw, grinning. "Didn't find no horse."

The knives were gouging away at his bones harder than ever. Carson set his jaw against the pain and knew his only chance was to prolong the trial as long as possible until he could control his hands, which now felt as if they were being put through a meat-grinder.

"How'd I get there?"

"Mebbe you rode one of yore cows," said Bearclaw, amused at the picture.

"Got one more charge against you," said King Fisher. "Horse-stealin'. We don't take that lightly 'round here. Where'd you get the horse you were ridin' when we got you down in Mexico?"

"Bought it."

"Where's the receipt?"

"I didn't ask for one."

"But you bought it?"

"Yes."

"Fair and square?"

"Ah," said King Fisher. "Fair and square, he says."

The bar of sunlight that had striped itself across King Fisher's silver and ebony gun butt had shifted a few inches lower to his holster. The butt itself was in shadow, and the small silver inlays glowed in the dark wood like small oblong moons. Carson asked God silently for ten minutes more of talk. That would suffice for his circulation to return. King Fisher had taken the cigar out of his mouth and was examining the end, savoring the cigar and the moment.

"You insist on that?"

"Yeah."

"Bring him in, Bearclaw."

Bearclaw went to the door and said curtly, "You! Come on in." The old miner came in.

"Recognize him?"

"Sure!" said Carson. "Ask him, he knows."

"Did this man buy your horse?" asked King Fisher.

"No," said the miner, pale.

"No what?"

"He stole it."

"How?"

"He stuck me up an' took it."

"How much he pay you for it?"

"Nothin'."

"Sure?"

"Yep," said the miner, staring at the floor.

Even in the midst of Carson's helpless rage, he felt some pity for the man.

"Anythin' to say to that?" asked King Fisher.

"Yep." Carson's cold casual tone brought King Fisher's heavy head up. He stared with renewed interest. He had been slowly turning Carson's pliers in his hands. He had been bored with Carson's lack of fight.

"Well?"

"I could take that witness," said Carson slowly, "an' prove that Jesus Christ ran a whorehouse on the San Miguel. Yessir, a whorehouse on the San Miguel."

King Fisher roared with delight. He turned to the old miner, who had flushed red. "Whaddya say to that?" demanded King Fisher.

The man stared at the floor.

"Whaddya say?" King Fisher persisted. "You been accused of perjury, man!"

The man swallowed and mumbled, "I done tole you, he stole my horse. An' my saddle, an' my Winchester."

"Well, let's add it all up," said King Fisher. "Trespassin'. Destruction of property. Murder. An' horse-stealin'."

"That's only four," said Carson. "How about larceny for the saddle an' Winchester? That'll make it a full house."

King Fisher chuckled. He looked almost affectionately at Carson, then turned to the jury, none of whom shared his amusement.

"Well, time for the verdict," he said. "Anyone see any reason why he ain't guilty?" Two of the jury were Mexicans;

they seemed sympathetic; their dark faces were not set in the tight manner of the others. But they said nothing.

"Well," said King Fisher, turning towards Carson, "we'll have to hang you. If you'd like to write a letter to any of your kin I'll see they get it."

"Got no one."

"All right, Bearclaw," King Fisher said. When Bearclaw was close enough Carson sank his left fist deep into Bearclaw's belly. It went in up to the wrist. With his right hand he pulled the ebony-handled Colt out of the holster. But his fingers could still not curl firmly around the butt nor could his right thumb pull back the hammer. Before he could bring his left hand across to fan back the hammer, his right hand was struck violently by his pliers, hurled by King Fisher as he lay in the hammock. The shock smashed the gun out of his hand. It fell in front of Bearclaw, who was kneeling on the floor and gasping in agony. Archie kicked the gun out of Carson's reach and smashed his Colt barrel against the side of Carson's head. He staggered sidewards against one of the upright beams. He held on to it while his head cleared a bit. He felt like weeping in rage. He felt some blood trickle slowly down his cheek and along his jaw. Head down, he watched a few drops drip off onto his torn and filthy shirt.

He was dragged outside and boosted roughly onto the wagon seat while Archie placed the noose around his neck. Carson was aware of details that he knew were unimportant but which seemed at the time to be very much so: several of the fibers of the riata were scratching his neck and he resented that indignity. He was still furious at his hand for betraying him and he still was not terrified at the thought of death—he was lucky that the scratchy rope and the barrel that had laid his head open prevented him from thinking about it. Dimly he realized that the rope had no hangman's noose on it. That meant he was to strangle to death instead of dying quickly with a broken neck. Archie managed to throw the rope around the wagon loops on his second try and pulled in his slack, whistling tunelessly. He was grinning, revealing his projecting dog teeth more than usual. The Mexicans crossed themselves and took off their sombreros. That gesture singled itself out from all the other things Carson was feeling and thinking as the surest sign that he was to die. He was so groggy from the blow that two men hopped up beside Archie and held him upright.

"All set, boys?" asked King Fisher.

Archie placed the flat of his palm in the middle of Carson's back, ready to shove him into the air. He nodded.

King Fisher walked over. Carson watched the slow, powerful steps coming closer. He prayed that King Fisher might get close.

"Anythin' to say?"

Carson looked down at him. One eye was rapidly swelling.

"You don't look so pretty yoreself," said Archie.

Carson ignored him. "Yeah," he said.

"Gonna beg, boy?" asked King Fisher, grinning.

Carson looked down into King Fisher's uplifted, hard, contemptuous face.

He spat into King Fisher's face and looked up into the cottonwood. It was full of fine white cotton from the seed pods, and a sudden puff of wind sent thousands of tiny flecks drifting among the green branches. Beyond the tree he could see a few old horses grazing on the rich grass, swishing their tails to keep the deer flies off. Beyond the horses rose the blue mountains. He knew it was to be his last look and he wanted a good one. King Fisher slowly wiped the saliva from his face, still grinning; this time he seemed pleased.

"Cut 'im down," he said.

"But—" began Archie, reddening.

"Said cut 'im down," repeated King Fisher gently. "Don't make me say it a third time. Give 'im some of yore clean duds an' loan 'im yore razor."

"But the jury found 'im guilty!"

"New evidence just came in," said King Fisher. "I declare a mistrial." He went back to his hammock, and sank back in it, lighting another cigar. "All right, boys, back to work," he said, ignoring the angry, vicious stares. Through the blue smoke of the Havana he stared thoughtfully at his cattle grazing across the valley, like myriads of speckled poppies. From time to time a tiny, amused smile settled on the corners of his mouth.

Chapter Five

Carson rubbed his left hand along his smoothly shaved face. He had not shaved for three weeks and he was not used to it. One of the Mexicans had shaved him since he was still unable to hold anything firmly in his right hand. Tito was very careful and had not cut him or irritated his sunburn. A neat piece of adhesive plaster covered the cut where Archie had clubbed him. His feet were clean and the blisters and cuts smeared with an ointment that made them feel better. He had eaten well, and he sat far back in an armchair under the cottonwood as dusk fell slowly from the ranges. King Fisher sat beside him in another armchair watching three old horses munching grass close to the wire.

"I pension off my old ponies an' let 'em enjoy a little peace an' free grass," King Fisher said. He leaned over and poured some bourbon into Carson's glass. "Where you from, Carson?"

"Kansas," Carson said. He was still a bit dazed from the good food he had just eaten and from the shock of still being alive. In front of him stood the two wagons. He looked at the wagon seat where he had stood waiting for Archie's vicious push in the small of his back. He rubbed his neck where the rough noose had left a small red irritation. He lifted his glass and took a long sip, sighing with pleasure.

"Kansas. Damned poor recommendation," rumbled King Fisher. "Damned poor recommendation!" He drank. "I been watchin' you, boy. I been checkin' up. You let me ramble on, I got a proposition. Don't interrupt me till I'm done talkin'. I come out to Texas when I was small enough to run under a chicken, but Uncle Asa there, he come out after the war; he used to be a big planter on the Tombigbee, had over three hundred slaves. When the war started he swore he could drink all the blood that would be spilled

31

in the war. But long befo' Sherman came his oldest gal was a ploughin' corn with the bull, an' his wife a bobbin' fo' catfish in a cypress swamp. We got good lines. What'd your people do, boy?"

"They farmed. Then my pa ran away, and my ma took in washin'. She died when I was thirteen. I drifted down here. I worked hard diggin' postholes, peelin' potatoes as a cook's helper. Then I started punchin' cows. Saved every penny. Bought five thousand acres no one else wanted. Bought thirty cattle to stock my range with. Was on my way back when I cut your wire."

"Been out here longern' you, then. We came out in a wagon, and we nooned at a little spring thirty miles north. I was seven years old. I went out into the bushes to do my duty when twenty Apaches hit the wagon. I didn't make no sound, I had that much sense. They killed my ma and pa fast. There were ten sacks of coffee in the wagon and they poured it on the ground. They smashed the crate with my ma's fine china and silver. They took my pa's sword, the one he wore in the war with Mexico, and broke it. I can still remember them Apaches breakin' the sword and cuttin' up the silver. I had sense enough not to cry. When they was gone I covered up my ma and pa with stones so the coyotes wouldn't get them and I thought, if this here country belongs to them Apaches, I was gonna take it away from them. An' if they wanna fight me for it, so much the better.

"I took some biscuits and I walked three days before I met some teamsters comin' from Santa Fe. They buried my people an' one of 'em sort of adopted me. When I was fifteen I struck out on my own and got a job with a small rancher near here, said he couldn't pay me but in cattle. I worked hard for one whole year. Then I wanted out. 'What's your brand gonna be, son?' he asked me kindly, and I never had thought about that, so I picked my initials, KF for Kirby Fisher. He cut out four old cows an' three scrawny calves from a run of range cattle, burned the KF on 'em, and threw 'em down on the mud flats. 'There's yore wages,' he said. Later I heard he was braggin' he had given me the first degree in the cattle business. Then winter closed in an' the pore old skinny bellies an' sway-backs died, they was fit for nuthin' but dogmeat, moanin' for help. An' I said to myself, there is another degree, the

Royal Screw degree, an' I will give it to him before I die. An' I did. I had to wait twenty-four years, but I gave it to him." He put more whisky in his glass and said, smiling, "You met 'im."

"Met 'im?"

"Why," said King Fisher, lifting his glass and sipping it as he stared coldly at Carson, "he's the man who swore you stole his horse."

Carson made his face impassive and said nothing.

"Once he used to run over ten thousand head. His house, why his wife had pier glasses she imported from Paris and she had a grand pianner she used to paw at in one of those Paris gowns. He had a couple sons. An' now, why, if I tole him to kiss my ass in front of the courthouse in high noon, he'd do it. I let him keep his little mine. I don't want him to starve to death. It keeps him goin' an' keeps him handy. Every once in a while I like to dust him off and let the four counties around this one know what King Fisher's Royal Screw degree is like."

The slow, cool wind which had been sliding down the eastern slope of the mountains and bending the tops of the grass reached the tops of the cottonwoods. The branches heaved and stirred. Clouds of the fluffy cotton broke free and drifted down. King Fisher placed a hand over his glass to keep them out of it.

"All right," he said. "Here's my proposition. I like the way you handle yourself. You came up the hard way, like I did. You think fast, you keep out of trouble when you can, when you can't you get into it fast, and you shoot first, an' you shoot careful. When yore luck is bad you don't crawl."

He lit a cigar and turned it slowly in his hand. "Yo're more like me than any of my kin. Bearclaw is so dumb he couldn't find his nose in the dark with his two hands a helpin'. Sendin' him or Archie to handle somethin' delicate is like tryin' to pour melted butter on a red-hot spoon up a wildcat's ass.

"I got a ranch here with the western border runnin' sixty-four miles in a straight line. I'm the first one in West Texas to run bob wire. I got so many gates between pastures that they hadda send me half a boxcar just full of gate-hinges. I got friends in Washington. I got somethin' big goin' here. I need someone to help me, it's gettin' too big an' I can't be everywhere at once. I need a good cattle-man, and he's gotta be a good man with a gun. I need someone who ain't afraid to break the law when he has to. But I don't want him lookin' for trouble, like that damn fool Archie. I need someone who speaks Spanish good, I got a lot of business with Mexico.

"I want you to learn how I do business. You can run yore cattle with mine. I'll keep tally for you. There won't be no calves missin' either. I know you cain't run yore spread the way you're runnin' it now—one bad winter and the bank'll take it back. Ain't no one gonna risk any more mortgages on yore little place. Yore next payment is due in two months. How you gonna meet it?"

Carson shrugged. "I'll meet it," he said.

"How? Gonna stick up a train?" said King Fisher. He blew some smoke. It was the same color now as the mountains.

"You don't have a cent in the bank," he went on. "I checked. You spent yore last dollar buyin' that piece of wolf-bait from Spencer. I know all about you, boy. If wild geese cost ten cents a dozen you couldn't buy a humming-bird's ass."

Carson grinned in spite of himself.

"First time I seen you smile, boy. I think we'll get along. Now, standard wages for a general manager for a spread this size is three fifty a month. I'm gonna start you at five hundred." Carson's eyes widened. He had never made over a dollar a day as a cowhand. "I'm gonna give you five percent commission on every deal you handle for me. You'll make that mortgage payment with one hand tied behind you. In two years you'll be able to buy that spread free an' clear and no one can take it from you then. Not even me. Two more years you'll be able to buy some damn fine bulls and some top heifers, and in five years from now you'll be breedin' cattle a hundred and fifty pounds heavier than any-one in West Texas—'cept me."

"Sounds fine," said Carson. "But I got a question. If you want me so bad, why pay me all that money just to have me leave in five years?"

King Fisher slapped his thigh, delighted. "Knew you'd ask! Because I want you to get so used to them wages you won't wanna quit. With that kind of money you could hire yourself a good man to run yore spread. Let someone else run that pokey lil outfit of yours, boy. Child's play! I got somethin' *big* to play with.

"I expect some of these days to stand up before my fire and shake off my Colt and Winchester an' kick 'em in an' watch 'em burn. I want someone runnin' this place then I can trust. An' mebbe you'll want to stay."

Carson's mind raced through its calculations: the wages, the mortgages, the prize bulls, the backlog in the bank to tide him through the bad winters that were bound to come, his feeling that King Fisher was telling the truth. The realization that Bearclaw and Archie wouldn't like it at all appealed to him. And if he didn't like it he could quit—and he would quit with several hundred or even a thousand dollars in the bank. He was a little drunk and knew he had better think out the whole thing very carefully before he committed himself. He set his glass down and thought.

"You look like a coon hound who ain't sure if the bear's dead or playin' possum," observed King Fisher, chuckling. "Well, boy, you just smell yore way round my proposition. Let me know in the morning."

In the morning Carson said, "All right." They shook hands on the deal. King Fisher said, "First thing, I want you to pick up some horses down in Isleta. You know where that is?" Carson shook his head. "It's down along the Rio Grande. You'll go along with my two Mex hands, they know their way around down there. I'll give you five thousand in twenty dollar gold pieces. They don't want paper money and silver'll be too heavy. The horses'll be wet."

King Fisher plunged his face into a big white basin set on a stand and washed. One of the Mexicans poured water from a white pitcher into the basin and stood back to get away from the splashing.

"Wet? What's wet mean?"

King Fisher pulled his huge dripping face out of the basin and stared at Carson as Tito handed him a towel. "Why, it means wet," he said heavily. "You'll have to take 'em just as they come out of the Rio Grande."

Carson stared at him.

"If you wanna back out, say so now," said King Fisher. He wiped his face, looking at his meadows as the cloud shadows raced over them. The faint contempt in his voice was obvious. " 'Cause you're gonna earn yore money with me. Yes or no?"

"Yes," said Carson.

Chapter Six

King Fisher rode with Carson and the two Mexicans as far as the gate. The Mexicans took off their sombreros and he shook hands with them. Then he shook hands with Carson. It was the first time he had ever done so, and Carson felt for the first time how hard the man's hand was. He could feel King Fisher's gold ring cutting into his knuckle as the man sat looking at his face with a half-quizzical, half-intrigued smile. *"Buena suerte,"* said King Fisher, and turned and rode back; he rode deep, four joints of his backbone below the cantle.

The Mexicans put on their sombreros, *"Quizás poco atrás de Dios, Don Keeng Feesher,"* said Tito. "Maybe a little after God." The two Mexicans showed no inclination to talk with Carson. They rode a little behind, showing him the necessary deference. They rolled cigarettes and talked quietly in Spanish. Once Tito pulled his carbine from its saddle scabbard as his horse shied from a coiled rattler that refused to give way. The first shot blew its head off.

"Despues de Dios mi Weenchester," he said, grinning and ejecting the used cartridge. He pulled a fresh one from his bandolier and inserted it as his horse edged away from the writhing coils.

Each of Carson's saddlebags carried a hundred and twenty-five twenty-dollar gold pieces. Each of the Mexicans earned thirty dollars a month. Carson felt sure that they were loyal to King Fisher. Why would he have sent them if he did not trust them? But two Mexicans in Mexico would, he felt sure, behave differently from two Mexicans in Texas. He decided to watch them.

The five thousand would be a temptation for him, too. It would buy him quite a nice spread in Mexico. He decided that the explanation was that King Fisher wanted every-

one to watch each other. He smiled to himself, admiring the
man's guile. He felt fine, his hand could hold a gunbutt
again, Archie's spare clothes fitted him well, and he was
pleased that his first month's salary would let him meet
the next payment on his ranch. The hot sun forced the
pungent aroma out of the sage. He was lulled by the soft
comfortable creak of the leather under him and he began
to whistle.

He had completely underestimated King Fisher. The man
was hard. He was complex. He had built himself a small
kingdom with his toughness and shrewdness.

There was no one in that part of West Texas which he
had carved out as his empire who dared challenge him.
Victory was his, but the taste of it had gone flat in his mouth.
For a couple of years he used to swing in his hammock, with
his spurs gouging out the same plank that Carson had noticed,
smoking his cigars and thinking. He slept badly. He could
not put his finger on what troubled him; part of it, he
knew, was the loss of his son; the rest of it he had not
been able to decipher.

One day he suddenly realized what his trouble was.
What had been exhilarating through all the earlier years was
not merely the acquisition of cattle or the rangeland which
kept ringing his first small ranch like growth rings on a se-
quoia. Nor was it the deference shown him whenever he went
to Austin or to Omaha or to Chicago.

What he loved, he realized, was the struggle itself with
the hard and savage men who wanted just the two things he
wanted: land and power.

In the beginning it was the occasional Apache or Comanche
war party that made every night suspenseful. When he had
built his fortress and had hired plenty of good men, the
cemetery on the ranch began to fill up with Apache graves
as well as others. After that the war parties began to avoid
his ranch: it was simply too costly in manpower. For the
last year not a single attack had been made on the old re-
tired cowpuncher who plowed the rich river acres for potatoes and onions with a carbine scabbard strapped to the
plow handle.

It took time for King Fisher to realize that he missed the
war parties. He missed the occasional defiant yell from the

ridge opposite and the scalp waved from the top of a long lance.

Then when the ranch began to grow, his new enemies appeared: the ranchers whose land he coveted. If they were poor they fought him themselves with their sons. If they were wealthy they hired gunfighters. King Fisher enlisted his kin, and for fifteen years the bitter silent war went on. A second cousin of his would be blasted with a shotgun from ambush, then someone would be caught branding calves. Savagely maintaining that the calves had been stolen from his herd (and frequently telling the truth, as King Fisher knew) the man would be hung within five minutes from a piñon branch if he had been caught in the mountains, or from two wagon tongues in flat country.

Without opposition the easy uneventful flow of days bored him. His life had lost its salt.

What he suddenly realized, watching Carson standing on the wagon seat with Archie's palm in the middle of his back, was that up there he had a man for whom he had been searching for five years without knowing it: a man who could give him a glorious fight.

Carson was tough, intelligent, a fast thinker—and a man with a ranch no bigger than King Fisher's when he himself had first settled there because the Apaches wouldn't like it. Carson's ranch was a nucleus. Since it was a nucleus it could grow. It could grow only at the expense of the other ranches next to it. And King Fisher owned or controlled all the ranch property surrounding Carson's.

If Carson could be nursed along with money, with a taste of power, with a knowledge of how to use both; if he could learn how to handle local and state law enforcement officers; if he were to be introduced to the right people with whom to deal in Austin: why, then, mused King Fisher, he might break away and go all out against him.

But only a rich and powerful man would put up a good fight.

Therefore King Fisher decided that it would become his job to see that Carson became rich and powerful. Carson must never find out that he would be gentled along for this purpose. A man like Carson would never stand being handled as if he were a toy, even if he were to become rich by it. He must feel that all decisions were his, and his alone.

And he must never find out why King Fisher wanted him so badly.

But since he was designed for such a high destiny, mused the grinning King Fisher as he swung gently in his hammock, he would have to pass a few severe tests. He would have to be tested in the field, as it were. King Fisher devoutly hoped that Carson would pass it with flying colors. The test was simple: he had ordered the two Mexicans to kill him as soon as they crossed the border into Chihuahua.

Chapter Seven

Carson woke to the sound of a sharp click. Across the small campfire he could see that Tito had just pumped a cartridge into his Winchester. He was raising it when Manuel placed a hand on his arm and whispered, *"Déjele descansar buen porque en un rato el va a comenzar su viaje por el otro mundo.* Let him have a good rest because pretty soon he'll begin his trip to the other world." Tito shrugged and lowered the carbine and rested it on his knees.

Carson's head was on his saddle slicker; underneath that his Colt lay in its holster. Luckily he was lying on his stomach. Very slowly his hand inched upwards under the blanket as the two men idly smoked. The Winchester was pointed towards him. He knew that any suspicion on Tito's part that he was awake would make him fire immediately. He heard a dry whirr. He kept his eyes closed since he knew that they were looking at him, and probably regretting what they were about to do. The sound was made by Manuel's spinning the cylinder of his .45 in his hand. Most likely, Carson thought, it was pointing at him. Infinitely slowly his fingers curled around the butt of his Colt.

He threw the blanket aside and came up shooting.

Tito half rose, took one stumbling step, and fell dead into the campfire. Reflex action made him pull the trigger. The shot seared Carson's neck. His second shot broke Manuel's right shoulder and knocked him backwards off the flat stone on which he was sitting. He scrabbled for the Colt in the darkness with his left hand. Carson kicked it out of range.

"Hijo de la chingada!" said Manuel, still on his knees. His useless right arm dangled as he made the sign of the cross, bowed his head, and waited. If it had not been for his asking Tito to give Carson a little more time Carson knew he

would be dead himself, still wrapped in his blanket. But
if he let Manuel live he would have an implacable enemy
for the rest of his life. Carson looked down at the man, still
kneeling, head bowed as if he were before some altar.
Then he fired.

"Where's them two Mexicans?" asked Damon Bond. He
leaned back in his office chair and let the gold coins slip
through his fingers as if they were poker chips. Carson looked
through the dirty plate glass window at the sunken and fiery
street of Isleta. The elaborately curlicued gold scroll letters
on the glass read "D. BOND RANCH PROPERTIES."

"We got into an argument," said Carson. Bond looked
at the thin, harsh face with the tight lips. He decided to
drop the subject. "Damn shame," he growled. "They was
good men. How you gonna take seventy-three pieces of wolf-
bait up to King Fisher's place all by yourself I dunno. Why-
n'cha try to get 'em back? I got no men to spare."

"When I take delivery of the horses I'll start worryin',"
Carson said. "Gimme a bill of sale."

"I don't give no bills of sale."

Carson pushed the stacks of gold into his saddlebag and
started for the door.

Bond stood up, his square pale face reddening. "People
round here don't behave like that to me," he began.

"You gonna give me a bill of sale?"

"Look, Carson," said Bond, staring at the cold face,
"didn't King Fisher explain things?"

"No."

"We go down into Mexico for stolen horses," Bond said
patiently, leaning against his battered desk with his white
hairless arms folded across his vest. "And sometimes we ain't
too particular as to whose horses we get. Lots of them
horses we get down there got brands registered up here,
sometimes as far north as Wyoming. So we figure it evens
out."

"It evens out for you, maybe. For me it don't even
out. Suppose someone wants to ask questions?"

Bond grinned. "Why," he said softly, "that's where a
couple good men like them Mexicans come in handy."

Carson looked without expression at Bond, who added re-
assuringly, "You jus' say you bought 'em offen me. I'll back
you up."

"No offense meant," said Carson, "but if they're gonna come to you to find out if I bought 'em from you, and you say you're gonna back me up, why not gimme the bill of sale right away? That backs me up and no time wasted telegraphin' you to check on my story. Or my neck don't get stretched by some overanxious deputy."

"Between here an' King Fisher's ranch you ain't gonna meet no overanxious deppity," said Bond. "No one round here is gonna risk stirring up that man."

"*Adios*," said Carson, and he walked out into the brilliant glare of a Rio Grande noon, the saddlebags slung over his shoulder. The town of Isleta, beaten flat by the white-hot glare of the sun, panted, crouching like a dog, waiting till late afternoon when it would rise to shake off the pitiless furnace in which it lay baking.

Most border towns on the Texas side were settled and built long ago by Mexicans. They were mostly Mexican in population and architecture. Even the signs were in Spanish—with an occasional exception, as Damon Bond's window. With that as proof, or with an occasional cowpuncher jingling by, the casual passerby could deduce he was in Texas. Else it was impossible to tell.

Isleta existed because a moderately good road led southeast to El Paso. A better one ran northward to the pueblo country of New Mexico. This road had been built in 1547. It was a good road for the transport of cattle to the Apache reservations where cattle were bought by the Indian agents.

To the south, once the river was crossed, another good road went through Saragoza, and then straight south to Chihuahua City, and thence to Mexico City.

Carson walked across the dusty street and threw the saddlebags over his horse. Before he had put his foot into the stirrup Bond was calling him back. When Bond had finished writing out the bill of sale Carson emptied his saddlebags once more. He asked if Bond could recommend two good men to help him drive his horses north.

In ten minutes Bond produced two men. One wore steel spurs. They were set close to his heels with a solid rowel three inches across. It would have the effect of a circular saw on horses' flanks.

The man said, "Sure makes them git a wiggle on theirselves."

"You bet," said Carson. He rejected the two men. He rejected two more men Bond produced out of a dark room at the back where they had been asleep. "Goddammit, Carson," said Bond, "I don't know what the hell you're lookin' for."

"Thank you kindly for your help, Mr. Bond," Carson said politely. He went to the nearest livery stable and had his horse fed and curried. He had done what he wanted: he had eliminated all the men recommended by a man who didn't like him. All others, then, would be men with whom he could deal on a fresh, unbiased level.

He asked a small Mexican boy working in the stable if he knew any vaqueros who wanted work. His two uncles were vaqueros, they lived in San Ildefonso, pretty close, would the señor wait till the evening? Carson waited. The two uncles came. They were in their forties, and had the shrivelled mahogany skin and calloused hands of old vaqueros. Their spurs had small rowels. Their horses looked good. When they pulled the saddles off and squatted for a talk Carson saw that the backs of their horses had no saddle sores. The saddles had high pommels and huge tapaderos on the stirrups. From the center of each cinch, under each horse's belly, hung a red tassel of horsehair. The men looked good to Carson. They said they would come.

Chapter Eight

"Bond give you any trouble?"

Carson shrugged.

"What'd he say about the Mexicans?"

"Nothin'. Just told him I got rid of them."

King Fisher grunted and came out of the hammock with the swift ease that always surprised Carson.

"Bond don't like me. Which means he don't like you. You bury them Mexicans?"

Carson shook his head.

"Plenty *zapilotes* around?" King Fisher was pulling on his boots.

"Yeah."

"*Zapilotes* might make people go over for a look-see," said King Fisher, "and if they find anything Bond'll hear about it."

"He never struck me as a man who cared what happened to a couple of Mexicans."

"Yeah," said King Fisher, "but if he don't like me, and if you wind up some day in Mexico he'll let them know. You ever been in a Mex jail?"

Carson shook his head.

"They don't feed you. Yore relatives feed you. If you don't have relatives you don't eat. But you won't be there long enough to get hungry. Because you'll be shot while tryin' to escape. Even if you ain't tryin' to escape."

"*Ley fuga?*"

"*Ley fuga.*" King Fisher lit a cigar. "Goddammit," he said without anger or passion, "an' I had somethin for you to do down there."

He looked at Carson. "Risky," he observed. "An' there's no one else who's got the sand or the brains for it."

"I'm takin' your money," said Carson.

45

"I ain't pushin' you, Carson. Think it over."

"I thought it over."

"You shoot them Mexicans this side of the river or in Mexico?"

"Mexico."

"Um," said King Fisher. "I want to show you somethin.' " They walked across the hard-packed yard. Scattered along the walls of the adobe were traces of the flower beds that King Fisher's wife had started and which he had let go to seed after her death.

He stopped in front of a low, strongly built adobe shed.

"Bond'll soon find out them Mexicans ain't been seen around any of those little river towns. That'll give him somethin' to chew on. He likes to sit there in that little office of his an' chew. He figgers sooner or later you'll be back Isleta way. Then he'll take out the cud an' look at it again. He's got friends in Mexico, too. They tell him things. I'm tellin' you, boy, you are gonna put your paw into a spring trap." He took a big key from his pocket and fitted it in a big padlock. "You sure you wanna go ahead?"

"I don't like Mr. Bond," Carson said. "I got an itch to see if he can close that trap fast enough to catch my paw."

King Fisher chuckled. Carson thought that he didn't seem too disturbed for a man who had just lost two good vaqueros. "You say the click of the carbine levers is what woke you?"

"Yeah."

"You sleep light."

"Lately I do."

"Yes," said King Fisher. "We must remember that."

He unlocked the door. The room was filled with wooden cases. Some were long, some were square. The long ones were marked SHOVELS; the square ones CHISELS.

King Fisher kicked one of the long cases. "Winchesters," he said. He kicked one of the smaller boxes and raised his eyebrows inquiringly at Carson.

"It ain't chisels, I bet," Carson said.

"You win a seegar," King Fisher said. "It's ca'tridges."

He locked up. When they were outside he said, "I ain't plannin' on startin' a war. But someone else is. An' he's gonna pay plenty for these. In the shape of cattle. You're gonna meet 'im in Saragoza."

"On the Mexican side?"

"Yeah. You wanna back out?"

"I ain't said so."

"If you get into trouble you better hit the Rio Grande at a
run. I'm sendin' Bearclaw with you. That sheriff's star might
carry some weight. Now come back while I tell you what to
do. An' you better pray they don't find out about you an'
them two Mexicans."

That afternoon the wagon was loaded. The cartridges covered the bottom of the big freighter. On top were the crates
marked SHOVELS. On top of that two men threw roll after
roll of barbed wire. King Fisher gave Carson a sheet
of paper.

It was a written order from Bond, on his stationery, asking
for a hundred and fifty shovels, crated in boxes of ten
each, sixty boxes of chisels, four dozen to a box, and fifty
rolls of barbed wire. The order was written in King Fisher's
handwriting. It was still wet, and he had come out of the
house waving it in the air. Carson folded the note carefully,
grinning.

"Bond's a much nicer feller than you think," said King
Fisher. "He gimme lots of these. The bobwire is to discour-
age casual look-sees. See if you can sell the stuff to Bond."

"After all," said Carson, "he ordered the stuff."

King Fisher slapped his thigh. "By God, he did, didn't he?"
he laughed, delighted.

Bearclaw sat silently on the corral fence, watching King
Fisher count out a thousand dollars in twenty-dollar gold
pieces. "Expense money," he said. As Carson packed the
gold into his saddlebags, King Fisher said, lowering his voice,
"I been watchin' Bearclaw. Funny as hell to watch that slab-
sided face of his thinkin' away. I can practic'ly hear the
gears clunkin'. He just can't figger you out. He's been like
that ever since he heard how you shot Tito an' Miguel. He's
a little smartern' the rest of my kin. That ain't sayin' much.
Reminds me of that ole Mex sayin'—'*En el pais de los
ciegos, el de un ojo esta el rey*'—you know that one?"

" 'In the country of the blind the one-eyed man is king.' "

"Yeah," King Fisher said, grinning. "Well, the others been
sayin' you kilt them two vaqueros o' mine in cold blood.
They been fixin' to get you."

"Why the hell should I shoot two men in cold blood? They
didn't have no money."

"Evvabuddy knows that. But you mighta shot 'em because

they was loyal to me. Until the night you caught 'em workin'
the levers of their Winchesters. If that's what happened."

"That's what happened."

"Yeah," said King Fisher. Carson turned to look at him.
King Fisher was looking at him and smiling. "Yeah," said
King Fisher, "that's what happened. I tole that to the boys.
But they wanted to cut you down, boy. None of 'em believes
you're loyal to me just because I saved you from bein'
hanged. Who put the rope around yore neck? Ol' King Fisher! So why wouldn't you reconsider the whole thing deep in
Mexico with all that gold to reconsider with? Eh? Why not?
That's what they said. So whajja do? You shot 'em in their
sleep. You told 'em you'd take the next guard and you shot
'em when you heard 'em snorin' away. Now, Carson, I ask
you, what's wrong with that thinkin'?"

"Why did I come back?"

"Who knows what lies in the heart of a man?" said King
Fisher, in the sonorous tones of an old preacher. "Mebbe
you figgered no one'd ever think you kilt 'em if you came
back. Mebbe you didn't want to live down in Mexico.
Mebbe you don't like *frijoles*. I sure as hell don't know. I
told 'em you did right. But you watch 'em all."

"I hear Archie's a good shot."

"That's right. Best I ever seen with a Winchester. He might
have pimples, but I seen 'im shoot the lock off the post
office door at a full gallop. He wa'n't fixin' to rob it, he just
took a bet he could do it. I hadda write a letter to the mar-
shal and the governor to make 'em forgit it. Damn fool
Archie can't make the distinction between a Fed'ral offense
an' somethin' like a State Land Office. They wouldn't kick
up hardly no fuss."

"I want him with me."

King Fisher was startled.

"Thought you didn't like cousin Archie."

"I don't. But I want a good shot along."

"You gotta watch him. He's snotty an' he'll try to pro-
voke you—an' he's fast."

"In Mexico I sort of figger on him sort of snugglin' up
to me for company."

"Yep. He'll go. He ain't gonna like it. But he'll go. When
you fixin' on leavin'?"

"Daybreak. Wanna get some things in town first."

"All right. Watch yore step."

Carson nodded and swung into his saddle. As he trotted out of the corral Bearclaw stared after him. King Fisher looked also. He was content. He thought that Carson was working out very well.

Chapter Nine

Carson opened his eyes and ran his hand through his newly clipped hair. It was his first haircut in months. The barber had smeared some oily pink grease over his hair just before he had combed it. It looked like pink sugar frosting and smelled like the usual Mexican whorehouse, but Carson liked it. He thought it was because on his very rare barber shop visits when he was still a child, the barber had given him lollypops after he had smeared the same pink grease on his hair. The barber massaged his scalp. Carson closed his eyes.

He felt very fine. He had just made a payment on his mortgage; he was wearing a new shirt and dungarees; the first sombrero he had bought in five years hung from the curved wooden hook on the opposite wall. His gun belt hung underneath the hat, weighted down by the heavy Colt. The leather in the belt was old and cracked: he had been in too many rainstorms and had swum too many rivers, and he had neglected to rub it with saddle soap too many times. He closed his eyes again and decided to get a new belt.

Steps came into the barber shop. They neared his chair and stopped.

"Gawd, he smells pretty," said Archie.

Carson kept his eyes closed. "My gun's on the hook back of you," he said. "Perfec'ly safe for you to shoot."

Archie's voice said, strangled with rage, "You think you're just the king bee 'round here, doncha?"

Carson still did not open his eyes. "You wanna talk to me, kid? I don't wanna talk to you. Why don't you take your big bad popgun and shoot at tin cans on fence posts an' pretend they're Indians?" He clasped his hands in front of him.

"He's callin' you, Archie!" Someone had yelled that from

outside the shop. "You gonna put somethin' in the kitty or are you gonna let him take the pot?" The barber slid his mirror to one side.

Carson heard him. He opened his eyes and said, "Leave that mirror there. I wanna see what you did." As he thought, Archie had obviously been telling his plans to the whole town. It seemed to Carson that just about everyone was standing on the board sidewalk staring through the filthy window. A potted fern which had died several years ago hung from the ceiling in front of the window. A few men had ducked low in order to peer underneath it. Bearclaw was nowhere in sight; Carson concluded this was because he would have to make some attempt to keep the peace. Carson closed his eyes again.

"Well, Archie," said the barber, disappointed, "look at 'im. He ain't even gonna open his eyes while you talk. That's downright disrespec'ful."

" 'Insolent' is the word you're lookin' for," said Carson, "and the word for you is 'stupid.' "

Archie grabbed the barber's dirty white sheet draped over Carson and jerked it to the floor. Carson still kept his eyes closed and his face impassive.

"That enough for you, yella belly?" Archie shouted. His hand hovered over his gun butt.

Carson opened his eyes. He completely ignored Archie. He behaved as if Archie were simply not in the barber shop. He looked in the mirror. He motioned to the barber to hold a small mirror behind him. He critically examined the back of his neck and passed his hand over it.

"Not too—" he began.

"I ain't gonna shoot you in the back, goddam you! Turn around!"

"—bad at all," finished Carson amiably. He grinned at Archie's furious reflection. He knew nothing serious would happen in front of the crowd as long as he was unarmed. He knew that if he were wearing his gun he was not sure what he might do. He preferred, therefore, to be without it.

"I ain't turnin' around," he said to Archie's reflection.

"What do I gotta do to make you draw?" Archie asked, almost plaintively.

"I'll put on my gun," he said, as if he were humoring a bad-tempered child. "Maybe I'll give you all the excitement you want. An' maybe not. Depends on how I feel. You treat me right, maybe I'll put it on. You talk bad to me, maybe I won't put it on. Maybe I'll just walk out of here backwards. You just gotta learn to be patient till I make up my mind." A few men guffawed.

Archie was no fool. He knew the longer Carson stretched out the situation the more ridiculous he would look. He spun around, grabbed Carson's gun belt and tossed it to Carson.

"Get goin', teacher's pet!" he said.

Carson held the belt in his left hand. He unbuckled it very slowly. Archie was trembling with impatience.

"You better sit down, Mr. Archie," Carson observed kindly, stopping his unbuckling.

He peered carefully at Archie. "Indeed you better," he went on. "You're gonna die of a stroke if you don't. This chair I'm settin' is mighty comfortable. Please take it, I don't mind standin' while I try to fix this here buckle."

He got out of the chair and politely stood aside for Archie.

"Come on, come on!" Archie said, his voice almost out of control, "you got that damn buckle open!"

"Ain't," said Carson.

Some more snickers from the men outside were like sandpaper on Archie's sensitive mood.

"Get it open, goddammit!"

"I wanna live a little longer," said Carson, in a plaintive manner. Everyone outside was grinning by now.

He very slowly spread the belt open. Archie watched every movement with almost unbearable intensity, clenching and unclenching his gun hand. Carson opened the belt wide. He stopped and poised the ends in the air, wide apart.

"Sure you don't wanna rest in the chair while you wait?" he asked solicitously, indicating the chair once more.

There was a loud chuckle from the crowd. Archie spun and glared at them. Then he turned back. Carson very slowly buckled his belt. He lifted his hands and poised them. Archie was tense and white.

"Wanna ask a question," Carson said, amiably.

Archie almost wept in vexation.

"Question is," said Carson seriously, "if I put my hands down in order to pull my belt one notch tighter, will you get excited?"

"Pull it tighter, Jesus Christ!"

Very slowly Carson put his hands down. He pulled the belt tighter.

"Reason why I want the belt tighter," he began conversationally, "is because—"

"I don't give a goddam why you want it tighter!" Archie shouted. "Just draw!"

Carson took his hands off the buckle. He placed both hands at shoulder level, opened and closed them a few times while he looked at Archie.

"You ready—" Archie began, but as the barber said later to King Fisher, "I never seed nothin' as fast. Archie had jus' about pulled the muzzle of his Colt offen the bottom of the holster by the time Carson had jammed his Colt about three inches deep into Archie's right ear. Archie he just stood there, froze, his mouth open like he was laid out in the back of Scanlon's parlour. He was so surprised he wasn't scairt. Then he thought a while and got scairt, so scairt he couldn't even swaller. I swallered. I was scairt it was the end of ole Archie, and him owin' me for five haircuts."

"What happened next?" grunted King Fisher.

"Carson whispered somethin' into Archie's other ear, I was the only one who heard it, because I was so close. He said, 'You can push a gun till you're dead,' and then he pulled Archie's Colt. Then he picked up the shavin' brush and he looked at the wet lather in the bowl, I swear for a minute he was gonna smear it all over Archie's face. Then he looked at Archie's face and smiled, and he put the brush back. Then he shook the bullets outa Archie's Colt and put it back in his holster. 'You can take your hands down,' he said, 'an' do me a favor, will you? Don't give your gun to anyone while I'm gone.'"

"Well, I thought the whole damn crowd would go into convulsions. Archie bust out, he picked up his hoss on those big Mex spurs he just bought, and shook him, an' when he set him down he was runnin' at his best, an' you could hear the rocks fallin' for minutes." He chuckled.

King Fisher said, "Archie's sure lucky. He better cool off, the crazy son-of-a-bitch. All he's got on his mind is to prove how tough he is. Carson don't have to prove that to anyone. If Archie pushes him once more I'm afraid it's gonna be another case of slow. But I got somethin' for him to do; hope it keeps him out of trouble. An' he might grow

up. Which he better do fast before he stops livin' completely."

It took the slow wagon two weeks to reach Isleta. Archie
was his usual sullen self. He had a filthy poker deck and in
the evenings he played solitaire until he was sleepy. Bearclaw, on the other hand, would ride ahead of the wagon.
If Carson happened to ride ahead Bearclaw would silently
drop to the rear.

One morning they found one of the mares of their remuda gone and a worn-out moccasin left in her place. Carson
knew it was a very clear message from the Comanche who
had stolen her that he was tired of walking. "We comin'
back this way?" Archie demanded. Carson said yes, it was
the shortest way. Archie said they'd have trouble and he
played no more solitaire in the evenings.

Bond was sitting at his desk when Carson finally walked in.
Before Carson could say anything Bond held up his hand.

"You bring the shovels an' chisels?"

"Yeah."

"Who you got to watch the stuff?"

Carson jerked his thumb. Bond got up and walked to the
window.

He sat down heavily and said, "Jesus. Those two."

Carson almost felt a surge of affection for him.

"If that's what you got, that's what you got," Bond said.
"King Fisher tell you what you're supposed to do?"

"Yeah. Saragoza."

"What else he tell you?"

"That's all."

"That ain't so good. Saragoza is where them two Mex came
from. The ones you fired." Bond underlined the last word
very slightly as he spoke. "It's been noticed in Saragoza they
ain't been back since they went through here with you. An'
they ain't written to their mommas either. I'd say right
off it wouldn't be too healthy for you to set foot anywheres
in Mexico for a spell." He smiled. "So I better handle the
deal myself."

"Pretty dangerous down there?"

"For you, yes. For me, no. I got friends down there."

"You get along."

"I get along, yes."

"You're supposed to introduce me to the man in Saragoza —that right?"

"That's right," Bond said, lazily.

"And the way things are, you figger I better stay here while you go over and fix everythin'—right?"

"Right. It'll be safer—"

"Yeah. I know. And you'll take the shovels and chisels along?"

"Nope. I ain't that dumb. That stays in Texas until we settle everythin'. Then we meet on an island in the middle of the Rio Grande twenty miles up or so. Then we start tradin'. So many cattle, so many Winchesters. Say he brings ten head across to Texas. I bring three carbines to Mexico. If they decide suddenly to double-cross us, not much harm done. See?"

"I see. Suppose you decide to double-cross him?"

"You don't do that around here an' live, Carson. There's too many clumps of blackjack oak or ocotillo to shoot from."

"Umm." Carson permitted a look of apprehension to sweep across his face. He then followed that with a look of relief. "Sounds safe that way," he said. "You sure you can deal with this rancher all right?"

"He ain't no rancher," said Bond, expanding under Carson's look of obvious admiration. "He's a general." Bond pronounced it the Spanish way. "All got up for the circus. Big sombrero with gold thread, charro pants with silver pesos flattened out and sewed along the seams, two cartridge belts crossed over his chest. An' he stinks."

"Stinks?"

"He never washes. I don't wash much, but he *never* washes."

"He a real general?"

"Hell, no. He's just a *bandido*. I can deal with him all right. I can handle almost anybody down there all right. Now take you, f'rinstance. You don't know nobody, you come in all alone, or mebbe with them two lightweights. An' then someone's bound to recognize you as the man who was down there with them two Mexicans who never was seen no more. An' you say you fired 'em. If you fired 'em so close to their homes how come they ain't been back?"

Carson knew enough to be able to find his contact.

"You're bein' a great help, Mr. Bond," he said.

It was obvious to Carson that Bond would like very much

to know what had happened to the two men. Since Bond had
not struck him as the kind of man who collected information
that he could not use, he must have a reason for wanting
to know. And when he found out, Carson was sure, he would
use the knowledge as a weapon.

"People come an' people go," said Carson, rising.

Bond shrugged, masking his irritation. "Nobody's seen
'em," he said.

Carson held out his palms and shrugged. He put on his hat.
"I guess I'll have to go to Saragoza myself," he said.

For a moment Bond's mouth hung open.

"Because," Carson went on, "I take the man's money.
I got to do what he says. He says I'm to go to Saragoza.
I'm goin'. Thanks for your offer."

He went outside. It was a little before noon. If he were
to leave now he could be across the Rio Grande and in
Saragoza by two, just after siesta time.

"I ought to be back by six," he told Bearclaw. "You better
stick by the wagon. I don't trust our friend too much."
Bearclaw grunted. Carson was pleased to see that Bearclaw
shared his opinion. As he headed towards the river he saw
Bond's face in the window. He thought, as his horse splashed
through the shallow water twenty minutes later, that the last
two people he had said good-by to in the United States would
be delighted if he were to die in the river or later that
afternoon in Saragoza. Bond made a good round trio. If he
were a Catholic he would have crossed himself, he decided,
and then, amused at the thought, he pulled a silver dollar
from his pocket, murmured "Good luck to me," and with
a flick of his thumb he spun it high in the air. It tumbled
over and over, its surface flashing the white hot sun at his
eyes. As it splashed into the warm clear water his horse
stepped onto the soil of Mexico.

Chapter Ten

Several children were throwing stones at a skinny brown dog as Carson rode into Saragoza. The dog walked patiently away, its tail curling between its legs and under its stomach. One stone hit it on the neck. It yelped and broke into a trot, its tail still curling in the same position. Carson put his horse between the children and the dog and told them harshly to stop. They stared at him, astonished. He waited until the dog had slipped between two low adobe houses. Then he rode on as the children stared at him, resentful.

He dismounted in front of a *pulquería*. It was called The Flower of Chihuahua, in flowery scrolls, above the double swinging doors that extended from shoulder to waist. A thick, old bougainvillea vine coiled above the doors, weaving in and out of a rusted iron balcony. Some of the red flower masses swayed above the doors.

Carson had to duck under the vine as he pushed through the doors. He sat down at a dirty table and ordered tequila. The bartender, looking as if he wished that it was Carson's throat he had under his blade, sliced a lime with a rusty knife. He placed a small saucer of salt in front of Carson with the tequila and the lime, and stared at Carson as he licked the salt, gulped the tequila and bit deeply into the lime. The liquor went down like a red-hot poker. He ordered another. It would not do to rush things when he wished to find out something.

There were four men at the bar. They had all turned around and were staring at Carson. They did not pretend they were not staring. It was quite unlike other places where Mexicans drank where Carson had been. The stares were icy and calm, not surreptitious and resentful. Carson had the feeling that they were about to move soon. He decided to

57

change his plan. Instead of waiting inside a place full of
hostile people he would do better to be out in the open—full
sunlight would suit him better than this dark corner. And
once outside he would be sure to stick close to his horse in
case it was advisable for him to leave town at a gallop.

Suddenly he saw several pairs of legs coming with a
quick purposeful stride towards the swinging doors. He pulled
out his Colt and placed it on his lap, under the table, out
of sight.

The legs stopped outside the doors. He put his hands in his
lap. Then he felt a ring of steel press the back of his neck.
Too late he remembered the little window that let in some
light.

"Manos arriba!"

He put his hands up.

The steel pressed viciously into his neck. *"Alto, mas alto,
cabrón!"*

He stretched them all the way.

"Pase!" called out the bartender.

The men outside came in. They carried Winchesters. One
of them handed his carbine to another, and coming close,
took Carson's Colt. Then he stepped back, examined it,
grunted with satisfaction, shoved it into his belt and took back
his carbine. He stepped over to the bar and leaned against it,
staring at Carson, as did all the others. No one said anything.
The steel ring was withdrawn from Carson's neck.

It was all professionally done, and Carson didn't like it at
all. He was a Texan, unarmed and in Mexico, and dealing
with men who knew what they were doing.

"Qué pasa?" Carson demanded, keeping his voice as unconcerned as he could. No one answered. He shrugged and
drank the last of his tequila.

He was not too alarmed. The men did not seem like a
lynch mob. He would ask for the general—when they found
out that he had come to speak to him, things would go
better. His problem, Carson knew, would be that he had
to ask for the general without getting himself into trouble with
any Federal troops—for the troops might be there searching
for the general.

When he contacted the general, that gentleman, figured
Carson, would protect him out of self-interest: his need for
the Winchesters and the ammunition would see to that.

More men arrived. A short, powerful man came in through

the doors. The others made way for him. He held a Colt in his hand. He pointed it at Carson and motioned for him to stand up, and Carson stood up slowly, measuring distances. The man made a little circle with the muzzle. Carson turned around and faced the wall. He judged that the man was not furious enough to shoot him in the back.

The man told three men to leave their weapons on the bar and search him.

Hands went through his pockets, ripping them completely. Three silver dollars fell to the dirty floor and rolled. His cigarette sack followed. Carson looked out of the little window through which the Colt had come to press the back of his neck. He saw four women sitting on a rough bench under a cottonwood tree. Three had the dark faces of Indian women, but the fourth woman, much more slender than the others, had a much lighter olive complexion. Her features were classically Spanish. When she put her *reboza* around her shoulders and caught sight of him, she made a start of surprise as she saw the men pointing their carbines at him inside the bar.

Carson was used to Indian women lowering their eyes to the ground whenever they realized that they were being looked at by him. Now when he looked at the woman she did not lower hers; she looked at him calmly and rose. The other women immediately rose also, and when she walked slowly away they followed her, very closely. Carson realized that they must be some kind of an escort. Unlike the barefooted women, with their dirty soles, she was wearing sandals. Her feet were clean. Under her long skirt she wore a clean petticoat—again, Carson knew that this meant she could not be Indian.

His intrigued musings were cut short by someone tying his wrists together with a piece of rawhide. He was pulled around and pushed into his chair. The fat man then came forward and pulled off his boots and examined them.

He grunted with satisfaction. Carson wasn't surprised: they had cost him twenty dollars and were the best pair he ever had.

The fat man then pulled Carson out of his chair, sat down in it, and pulled on the boots. They fitted well. He grinned with pleasure and kicked his old *alpargatas* aside. Then he crossed his thick arms and looked at Carson.

Carson was sure now that some official, probably this one—

maybe, Carson thought, he was a border official or perhaps a sheriff or deputy—had found out that Carson had come into Mexico to deal with a bandido. He would be questioned, Carson was sure, as to his intentions in crossing the Rio Grande. After a day or so, and a fat bribe into the fat hands of the fat official, Carson thought with some annoyance, he would be released.

The important thing was to make sure that he would not be shot in the first half-hour after capture while performing the time-honored shot-while-attempting-to-escape routine. He did not see how he would escape if the fat man decided to execute the *ley fuga*, but at least he could keep his ears and eyes open.

"What are you doing here?" asked the man, in Spanish.

"I'm here on business. Are you the sheriff?"

The man smiled. The crowd roared in amusement. He turned back to Carson.

"I'm the sheriff. What do you want?"

"I don't want to waste your time or mine. Where's the sheriff?"

"You don't have any time left, *amigo*. Consider me the sheriff and answer my question."

Carson deliberately turned his back on the man. He now faced the rest of the men. One of them slowly drew his forefinger across his throat.

"Why not?" dryly announced Carson.

The man stared at him, astonished. He had expected a show of fear or of defiance. The fat man flushed. He rose and grabbed Carson by the elbow and spun him around, but stopped when a voice called from outside the swinging doors, "Enough, Pablo."

Carson was shoved roughly outside. One of the men had taken Carson's sombrero and had clapped his filthy old one on top of Carson's head. It was a bit small, but Carson was grateful for the protection it would give him against the sun of Chihuahua. He was shoved just as roughly onto his horse. He looked for the man who had called out for Pablo to stop. Whoever it was had disappeared. The men seemed to be waiting for someone now.

Finally a man came out of a low adobe restaurant across the street. He was eating a tortilla from which some black beans were dripping. He gulped them, wiped his mouth with the back of his hand, and belched. All this time he stared at

Carson with an intelligent, calculating and sour eye. He was about thirty, Carson judged, and seemed to be deferred to by all the men present. They were waiting patiently for him to swallow his food.

He stepped back inside the restaurant and gave a curt order. The four women Carson had seen earlier came out. In the middle, with long easy strides, walked the girl. As they passed she looked at the man with a stare of cold, reserved hatred. He seemed to be waiting for it, and he burst into laughter. His hair was black and he needed a haircut. He wore the shaggy black mustache customary with Indians. The Indian woman who ran the restaurant came out with a tortilla in one hand and a sombrero lavishly embroidered with gold thread. He put it on with one hand while he ate the tortilla. For the first time Carson noted that the man was wearing charro trousers with silver pesos that had been flattened and bent to follow the curve of the legs.

He mounted a fine horse and came alongside of Carson—and as he expected, the whiff of the man's unwashed skin hit him almost like a blow.

"Oye, Tejano," he said.

"I want—" began Carson. He had started to say that he wanted to talk quietly to the man about a shipment of shovels, but he had gotten out only the first two words when the Mexican slashed him across the face with his quirt. It burned like a drench of acid.

"I talk, Tejano. You listen. Comprende?"

He spoke in English. "I—" began Carson again. He knew he had to talk fast before they pulled him out of the saddle and shot him. The quirt slashed him again.

"You got no time to talk, Tejano," said the man, lazily. "Me, I got time. I'm a general. You know what a general is? That's me. I'm half-Yanqui, half-Spanish. Me, I can't never be cavalry officer in Mexican Army. So I make myself my own general. Pretty good, huh?" He translated for his men, who roared.

He turned to Carson and demanded, "Hey, how you like my Eenglish?"

"You talk it better than me." Carson's glance roved up and down the man. A hundred yards in front rode the scouts, a hundred yards in back the rear guard. He counted a force of fifty or so, all tough, thin, with the big sombreros of the North. All carried machetes. About a fourth of them carried carbines. Carson noticed that their cartridge belts were only a third full. They had an easy, practiced, professional air about them.

"I talk it better than you? I don' know if I theenk that's fonny."

He frowned a moment. He lifted his quirt and thoughtfully rubbed his mustache with it. Then he chuckled.

"I work three years in Texas," he said. "All over the Big Bend. One day I get tired of people callin' me dirty Spik. So one night I kill my foreman and come across the Rio Grande—" here he clicked his tongue several times in succession and slapped each leg of his charro trousers several times with his quirt, pantomiming a fast ride.

"But before that I get to know plenty big people in Texas. Hey, how you like my pants?"

The general looked fondly at the rows of the silver pesos. "Pretty good for an Indian, no?" He caressed the rounded surfaces of the pesos. I took 'em offa *hacendero* in Sonora." He pantomimed firing a carbine. "Against a wall, boom, boom!" He rode in silence, his face brooding.

Then he brightened. "Same hacienda where my father was a peon. This *hacendero* he took my sister. Oh, she was pretty. He told my father not to poke around askin' what happen to her. My mother she cry a lot, so she went to the big house to ask. He hit her with a whip. I was maybe ten, eleven, I ran away. I come back fifteen years later with two hunnerd fifty men. My mother and father were dead, no one heard of my sister for years. I kill the *mayor domo* very quick. He didn't deserve to die so quick, but he was a very good man with a carbine and a knife. I had to have quiet. I pulled the *hacendero* out of his bed. He still up to his old tricks, he had a girl; maybe fifteen years old, in bed. Next morning I call all the peons together to watch. His wife was dead a long time, too bad. His daughter in a convent in Paris, too bad. At sunrise I drive a knife through both cheeks and through his tongue because he kept sayin' bad things about me an' my friends. Then I made a hole in his nose and put a chain through an' I led him around like a burro. Oh, he was stubborn!" The general chuckled at the memory. "But he followed. After a while we got tired of that. Then I cut a little piece off each finger. That takes till noon. We Yaquis very good about things like that. Peons getting bored. Then other things. After he died I say to the peons, what you think the government do to you for not stopping me? Eh? They will do the same to you. True? They agree. So I ask, where is safety? With me. Always moving, always with good guns, plenty of cartridges, when we take another hacienda plenty good clothes for the women, maybe good silver candlesticks from the chapel. So, my army grows. It is not hard. Plenty mountains to hide in, plenty deer. Plenty rocks to roll down on the Rurales.

"And one week after we kill him, who you think comes? His daughter. She came in a coach, with an escort of six soldiers. We kill the soldiers, fast, fast! I got the girl. She wait. Some day I take her like her father took my sister. But she don' like to wait—and that's why I want her to wait. I learn one thing in my life—waitin' for a bad thing to happen is worse than it happen right away. Si, Tejano! I don't know why I talk to you so much. Maybe because you got *cojones*, comin' here alone, a *Tejano*, into Chihuahua. An' after what you done."

Carson didn't like the sound of the last sentence. He pretended that it had no special meaning as far as he was concerned, but from the level, savage stare that the general was giving him from under the broad brim of his sombrero he knew that his life was hanging on a very thin thread. The general had pronounced the sentence slowly and sadly, almost as though he were a judge announcing a verdict.

"You kill two Mexicans last time you was down here," he added heavily. "I'm gonna take two, three days to kill you. I don' wan' no arguments, no talk. *Comprende?* Finish." He rode ahead.

Ten minutes later they came to a little muddy river with steep banks. Carson's horse hesitated a moment, and Pablo suddenly lashed her buttocks with his quirt. She leaped, kicking wildly at Pablo's horse. She fell on her side and slithered to the shallow bottom, pressing her rider into the foot-thick mud. His head was under the mud surface and he held his breath. Pablo chuckled as the mare slipped and struggled, trying to stand erect. Each time she fell she pressed Carson deeper into the mud. Since it was so thick he was unhurt, but he was suffocating and it took all his will power to keep from screaming for help. The general trotted back and watched, amused, with the rest of the men.

The captured girl jumped off her horse and into the mud. She grabbed Carson and pulled him erect, heedless of the mud

that covered her. He had just time to gasp his thanks when
the general put his horse in the water and slashed her face
with his doubled-up riata. She tried to grab the riata but
he held it aloft and laughed, whirling it around and around
his head as he fended her off easily with his other hand.
Carson set his teeth in his helpless rage and then he began to
vomit water and the mud he had swallowed as the horse
was rolling on him.

He was roughly shoved into his saddle. Pablo pulled out
Carson's carbine, wiped the mud from it, looked at it lovingly, looked warily at the general, and reluctantly thrust it
into the scabbard. Carson knew that the general must have
marked it for himself. But he was so nauseous with his retch-
ing that he had lost interest in everything.

After a spell of heaving he brought his head up and
saw her riding among the female escort while they slapped
and shoved her. She refused to wince or turn aside from the
blows. Carson, even in his nausea, began to admire the cool
arrogance with which she flaunted her indifference to her
muddy appearance and the red welt on her face.

Two hours later Carson suddenly recognized where he
was: a month before he had camped with Tito and Manuel
very close to this road. The air smelled bad. Carson was
pulled off his horse and shoved through the chaparral. He
saw the ring of stones which marked his old campfire.
There was the square-shaped flat stone on which he had
rested his feet while he ate. He had rolled himself in his
blanket near it; and there, close to the cholla, was where he
had heard the dry clicks of their Winchesters as they levered
cartridges into the chambers. Twenty feet further on was
where he had dragged their bodies and stripped them for
the *zapilotes*.

"You don' like the smell? Tha's too bad," said the general
as he looked at Carson's face. "Get off." Carson had never
dismounted from a horse with his wrists tied behind his back.
He hesitated, trying to figure out how to do it. The general
spurred his horse and the impact against Carson's horse sent
him sprawling off on the far side. One spur caught in the stirrup; his horse had started to shy away from what he obviously
thought was a crazy mount, but since he was well-trained
he stopped as soon as he realized Carson's spur was tangled
in the stirrup.

He lay helpless on his back, looking straight up at the sky. He was beginning to feel terrified now; he felt quite sure that nothing would deter the general from his desire for revenge upon any Texan for the indignities he had suffered across the river, or from the revenge he felt he must take from Carson for the two murdered men.

Carson, lying on his back, with his ankle twisted in the stirrup, was trying to think very fast how he could possibly persuade the general that he had killed the two in self-defense. Under the huge sombrero the general's dark face stared down at him.

A woman's hand reached into Carson's upside-down angle of sight and pulled his foot out of the stirrup. He struggled to a sitting position and stared up into her blue eyes. At first he had thought she was one of the Indian women, but then he saw she was the same woman who had helped him at the river. Carson did not know then that over three hundred and fifty years ago Pedro de Parral, one of Cortes' officers in the Conquest, had been awarded one-fourth of the state of Sonora. He had taken an Indian girl as wife. Much to the amazement of the other Spaniards, de Parral had his priest marry them. Ever since the Parrals had gone to Spain to find their wives and to bring them back to the great hacienda for the wedding in the Parral's private chapel.

In every way she showed the strain of the Conquistador—the way she held her head, her walk, the bone structure of her face. Only the olive complexion and the blue-black lights in her hair recalled her Indian forbear.

He struggled to his feet and stood, feet thrust apart in the middle of the red trail in the ocean of dusty grey chaparral. The general, sitting cross-legged on the ground with his carbine across his knees, watched him.

"*Tejano*," he said, "you don' like me?" He chuckled. He lit a cigarette and motioned. One of the *bandidos* brought up a pick and shovel, and threw them at Carson's feet. The general looked at the ground critically. "I think there," he said. He pointed with a dirty forefinger, leaned back and said, "We are waitin', *amigo*."

Carson slowly began to dig.

"Tell me," asked the general curiously, "why didn't you cover them with rocks, eh? No coyotes. No *zapilotes*. Nobody find 'em. *Tejano*," he finished, shaking his head in mock dismay, "you stupid, no?"

Carson said nothing but he silently agreed. He had thought the *zapilotes* would have disposed of the bodies very quickly, as they usually did. He had not been in any mood to spend an hour carrying rocks lest someone find him——he knew that almost everywhere, even in the most obviously uninhabited places he had come across narrow little trails. It now seemed to Carson that he would have done much better to have wasted that hour, even at the risk of being discovered.

He dismissed the regret from his mind and dug slowly and carefully, thinking quickly. He was becoming very thirsty as he dug in the hard-packed earth, in the full open sun. Without a sombrero the sweat ran into his eyes and the salt burned. From time to time he straightened up and wiped his face with his sleeve.

"You got a good grave, I like the way you dig. Nice square corners," said the general. Carson squatted, rubbing dust onto his palms for a better grip on the pick.

The general said, "Your good friend Señor Bond sent me a message las' night." Carson stared at him.

"He told me where to find you. Ah, Pablo, look at him! I told you he don' like that!"

Carson tried to make his face impassive again.

"Bond has been very useful to me. We are good—friends is not the word. No. We do business together. You think if I kill you how will I get my Winchesters? Eh? *Verdad, hombre?*"

"That's just what I'm thinkin'," said Carson. "Because you ain't gonna get 'em. Not from Bond, you ain't."

"*Porque?*" asked the general with a wide grin.

"Because he's gonna do what King Fisher wants, even though he don't like King Fisher and don't like me. He ain't stupid like you think he is."

The general grinned and translated for Pablo.

"So?"

"So," said Carson, "the only way you get your Winchesters is to send me back." He leaned on his pick. He had dug a foot out of the hole and his face, from the unaccustomed exposure to the sun without a sombrero, was seared a dull red.

The general looked at him slowly, up and down, savoring the moment.

"*Hombre,*" he said, "I don' have to do nothin'. *Comprende?* You come down to Mexico, you go in alone to a Rio Grande town, you got *cojones*, all right, but when you get killed no one gives a damn. *Verdad*? You know what you gonna get when you come down. You think I go alone to Texas? I go with lots of my frien's. Bond sees you don' come back. He finds out you been killed. So he takes the Winchesters and he makes the deal with me. The way King Fisher wants it. So what happen then? King Fisher says, well, poor Señor Carson, nex' time I go down Saragoza way maybe I drop some roses into the Rio Grande for him, or maybe I buy some candles for the church for him. Oh, he dunno I'm gonna plant you in a grave. Tha's somethin' you don' deserve, but you got *cojones*, hombre, that I do for you." He stood up suddenly, struck by a new idea, and thrusting his carbine high in the air and shaking it in his enthusiasm, he said, "An' one more thing! You wan' to write a letter to your mother, I let you! An' I see it gets mailed across the river."

One of the men had hacked branches off a mesquite and, using a rawhide thong, had made three crosses. He tossed them beside the head of the grave.

"See, *amigo*," said the general, "I like you. You get one. We ain't Comanches."

Carson dug on. "Smooth, very good," said the general approvingly. "I like the way you do it." He sliced his palms vertically in the air. "No hurry. I want a good grave for them two vaqueros you shot in the back."

Carson lifted his sweat-soaked face. His sombrero had floated off down the river when his horse had slipped in the mud. "Never shot no one in the back," he said.

"Sure, *hombre*. Hole plenty deep, *amigo*."

For ten minutes more Carson worked. When he had the edges as smooth and square as possible he straightened up.

"Finished?" asked the general.

"Finished."

The general stood up and threw away his cigarette. He pumped a cartridge into the chamber of his carbine. Several of the men, lounging in the shade of the mesquite, sat up and crossed themselves.

"Out," said the general, motioning with the muzzle of the carbine.

Carson climbed out. "How about one for me?"

"Sure," said the general. He reached into his pocket and pulled out a tobacco sack and some cigarette paper. Carson started to walk toward him.

"No, *chico*, no," said the general, almost regretfully. He swung the muzzle towards Carson's heart. Then he thrust a match and a cigarette paper inside the sack, and tossed it to Carson. Carson made his cigarette, lit it, and decided it would be no use to walk toward the general to offer him the sack. He tossed it. The general caught it and grinned.

Carson smoked the cigarette slowly, standing in the middle of the dusty grey chaparral.

"Do you believe in God?" asked the general.

"Not specially," said Carson.

"What is 'specially'?" said the general, displeased. Carson shrugged and took a long slow drag. The general still looked irritated.

"I mean—" Carson began. "I mean—" He decided he could not define the word. "Oh, hell," he said. "Just say the answer is no."

"Me," said the general, "I believe in God. But I don't want to go to heaven. Heaven is for the stinking rich Mass-goers in Durango and Chihuahua. I want to go where a man like Juarez went. Tell me, *Tejano*, where did Juarez go?"

Carson shrugged.

"Tell me," demanded the general, "where did Juarez go?"

"*Quien sabe?*" said Carson, and threw his butt away.

"All right. Stand in the grave."

Carson did not move.

"The grave!"

Carson still did not move. He would have to be forced into the grave; some one would have to come near him for that, and that, he knew, would be his last chance.

"*Vete!*"

Carson set his teeth and stared at the general. The general spoke a sentence in Spanish too swiftly for Carson to catch. Several men put down their carbines and took off their knives and revolvers. They they came toward him from several different directions. Carson waited, on the balls of his feet, his hands half-clenched. It would be six to one. Two came to the edge of the grave, on the other side away from him. They started to step down into it. They dropped their eyes for a fraction of a second. Carson jumped into the grave and jerked an ankle out from under each man. They went sprawling, but three more had launched themselves at him from his rear. He had expected that and was ready, fighting with his fists and teeth and elbows.

Two were half-paralyzed from blows in the solar plexus and doubled over, one man held a nose from which blood was pouring. From the corner of his eye Carson could see the general watching with not a sign of alarm. He even lifted his cigarette for a puff with a look of amused interest. It all gave Carson the feeling that he was simply supplying a brief interlude for the general's day. Nevertheless he fought on, panting. Two more men ran up, one with a Colt stuck in his belt. Carson saw it, but two arms went suddenly around his neck from the rear. He broke the grip by falling on his knees and bending forward. He fought erect and plunged at the man with the Colt.

A riata dropped over his head and tightened on his arms. He started to work it loose; another riata dropped over his head and tightened across his arms and jerked him sidewards to the bottom of the grave. He struggled to his knees and started to rise when a third riata settled over his neck and tightened. He couldn't raise his arms high enough to loosen it. A roar like a waterfall filled his ears as he fell backwards, unconscious.

Chapter Eleven

Carson heard the sound of a hammer as he struggled upward to consciousness. He found he had been propped up against a tree. A riata still bound his elbows to his sides. A rawhide thong held his wrists together. Someone had spilled water on it; the result was that it had shrunk so tightly that his hands felt numb. The general was still sitting where he had been, with his carbine still across his lap.

Carson's throat felt sore. He swallowed what little saliva he could assemble: his throat hurt quite badly when he swallowed. The hammering went on. He turned his head. His saddle lay upside down on the ground and a man was hammering spikes into the cantle so that the points stuck two inches beyond the leather inner lining. The wooden saddle tree held the spikes firmly in place.

He stared, bewildered. The whole thing seemed pointless and he craved some water; the effort of turning to see where the hammering was coming from made him groan with pain. He realized then that his whole body was badly bruised.

The general saw that Carson was again conscious. He nodded. The saddle was thrown over the horse, cinched, and four men set Carson into the saddle. He pressed forward to escape the sharp points of the nails. By arching his back to its maximum he found that the points just grazed the base of his spine.

One of the men mounted and tied his riata to the horse's reins. Then they all moved a quarter of a mile down the road, where Carson remembered there was a large flat area. When they reached it the man leading Carson's horse stopped and looked at the general.

The general thrust several cartridges into his carbine till it was full. Then he nodded. At the end of thirty feet of riata Carson's horse trotted obediently. The man spurred his

70

horse. By the time he had reached a fast trot, the arch of Carson's back could not protect him any more. He was bouncing too much and the sawing motion was raking his skin. He tried to lean forward; he could see the general lifting his carbine. Carson thought savagely that when the bullet hit him it would blast him out of the saddle and that the horse would drag him, unable to stop with the man at the other end of the riata forcing him. He hoped the bullet would kill him quickly. He braced his body for the shock of the bullet.

The crack of the Winchester in the desert air sounded flat and without menace, almost like a cheap firecracker. Its passage not six inches from his face pushed the air against his cheek. He saw the general grin as he ejected the shell. He had missed deliberately, Carson knew, and that took as much skill as hitting him as he moved.

"Pronto!" called out the general. "Mas pronto!"

The vaquero broke from his fast trot into a gallop. Carson's horse obediently followed. It was no use to lean forward to try to escape from the spikes—the speed at which he was now moving ground the points in a vicious rowelling movement against his lower back.

The general fired again; this time the bullet passed a few inches back of his head. Carson knew that if the general were judging his distances correctly in order to miss him so closely, he would be killed if he were to suddenly move his head a few inches to the front or to the rear. He would have to remain in one position, and that with the spikes digging into his back.

The game went on for ten more minutes. Pablo was allowed to fire a few shots. Then the general tired of it. Three men tore Carson roughly from his saddle. The pain in his spine caused by the spikes was so bad that he almost cried aloud.

Pablo drew out his machete and ran his thumb along the edge. A thin red line appeared on the dirty skin. He held up the bleeding thumb, grinned, and ran it along his throat.

Carson was half-dragged, half-carried to a cottonwood branch lying on the ground. Its top had been shaped by machetes until it was V-shaped. He was made to stand barefoot on the sharp edge. Three men held him while four others, using their combined strength, pulled his legs as far

apart as they could, until he thought his tendons would
crack. Then they securely tied his feet to the branch.

His wrists were still tied behind his back. A riata was tied
to the thong and tossed over a branch directly overhead.
Three men pulled downwards on the riata. The strain caused
intense pain. The tendons of his arms and legs were severely
strained, and the spinal column bent so that he felt as if it
would break in two any moment. His shoulder blades were
forced into close contact, pressing the vertebrae inward. Wave
after wave of excruciating pain flowed from the base of his
spine, which had been lacerated from his ride in the spiked
saddle.

Because of his position Carson's head was bent forward. A hand grabbed his hair and jerked his head upward.
The general was there, looking at his face with mock
solicitude.

"You all right, *Tejano*?" he asked. "You sick, maybe?"

Carson said nothing. After a moment the general let his
head drop onto his chest.

"Don' worry, *Tejano*," the general went on, "you came to
Mexico to see me, I give you somethin' to look at."

Another hand grabbed Carson's hair and his head snapped
backwards. He felt a wave of heat pulsating from something—for a moment he thought it was the sun, since it came
from directly overhead.

Then he saw. It was a white-hot branding iron. Pablo was
holding it and rolling it back and forth. "This one is hot,
Tejano," said the general. He bent down and picked up a
dried twig and touched the iron with it. It shrivelled to a
twisted grey ash; a wisp of acrid smoke curled upwards.

Carson saw that the brand read LIPM.

"*Libertad Y Independencia Para Mexico*," said the general. "My brand. For my cattle. You came to Mexico to see
what business you could do with me, no? I show you. With
Libertad y Independencia, I close your eyes." He motioned
to Pablo.

Pablo, grinning, raised the iron and slowly brought the
white-hot letters closer and closer. He held it one inch from
Carson's eyes.

Instinctively he kept them as tightly closed as he could.
The heat was so intense that it seemed to Carson that his
eyes were being dried up like an alkali flat. His nose felt as
if it were on fire.

The time seemed to Carson to run on and on, but it lasted less than half a minute. The heat went away, the hand released his hair and his head fell forward. When he lifted his aching eyelids he saw everything as through a red mist. His left eye ached and throbbed, and every few seconds it seemed as if something passed in front of it, darkening his vision. Carson thought for a moment that someone was holding a hand in front of his eye deliberately, but then he realized that no one was there.

With the right eye he could see fairly well, except that everything seemed red instead of its usual color. The hot iron had been thrown down and was frizzling on the ground a few paces in front of him.

Carson's horse had been tied to an ocotillo branch near him. She was nibbling at the crimson flowers of the ocotillo and was very unconcerned with what was happening to Carson. Through the red blur which was almost the sum total of Carson's sight he saw Pablo pulling the Winchester out of Carson's saddle scabbard. It had been lying in the sun, and the mud which had seeped inside when his horse had slipped crossing the river had dried almost as hard as adobe. Pablo pulled it out, freeing the barrel from the dried mud, and hefted it with pleasure. He liked the weight and the balance, Carson saw.

Pablo pumped a cartridge into the chamber. He hefted it once more. *"Para mi, general?"* he asked.

The general nodded. Pablo nestled the stock against his cheek and pointed the carbine to the harsh blue sky.

Carson was sure there was dried mud inside the barrel. He watched as Pablo rubbed his cheek fondly against the stock. He squeezed the trigger.

The muzzle burst. The carbine turned a somersault in the air. Pablo fell backwards to the ground, where he remained on his back, bleeding badly and screaming like a child. His nose was broken, one eye was gone, and several of his front teeth were shattered, and he was holding both dirty hands to his face, writhing and kicking at the men who were trying to pull his hands away. Carson could not help showing his satisfaction.

The general looked at him. "You like it, *Tejano?*" he said. "Tomorrow we see if you laugh. *Buenas noches.*"

Chapter Twelve

"This Mr. Bond," said Archie, looking between the breasts of the girl who sat in his lap. Somewhere in the whorehouse a clock struck one. "This Mr. Bond," he repeated. The yellow glare of the kerosene lantern hanging on a hook set in the adobe wall made her look almost pretty.

"Yeah," said Bearclaw, lifting his fifth full glass of bourbon.

"This Mr. Bond," said Archie with finality, rubbing the girl's naked shoulder till she winced.

"Spit it out!" said Bearclaw, setting his glass down carefully. "Spit it out, goddamit! I don't know, but I can't drink no more till you spit it out. Yo're curryin' that gal like she's a horse."

Archie stood up abruptly. The girl slid between his legs and hit the floor. "*Hideputa!*" she screamed.

Archie went outside, stumbling from table to chair to wall to door. After a minute he returned, staggered inside, and fell into his old chair. The girl promptly sat in his lap again and squeezed his neck in an embrace.

"Whereja go?"

"Where the hell didja think I went?" Archie said, without heat. He filled another glass and said, "This Mr. Bond is sutinly good to us, ain't he?"

" 'On the house!' he said," stated Bearclaw, waving his glass in a grand gesture, spilling it over the girl's skirt. She jumped up once more and screamed at him in rage. She backed off against the wall and wrung out the skirt, still simmering.

"These Mex girls sure get excited easy," said Bearclaw. "Bourbon on the house! Gals on the house!"

"Yeah, that's right," said Archie. "He's real nice. But you

74

ain't nice. I ain't nice. What I mean is, why should he be nice to us? Hey?"

"Aw, shut up an' drink. Worry about it in the mornin'. All by yourself. I'll be cuddled up with a hangover."

"No. Le's worry about it now. Carson didn't come back by sundown. Right?"

"Right!"

"So somethin' happened. Right?"

"Son-of-a-bitch is dead. Le's celebrate. Le's celebrate free!"

"Yeah, le's celebrate. But first you better think."

"Why do I gotta think?"

Archie said to his girl, "You speak English, baby?"

"No," she said. "Me no spik Eenglish."

"Sure," said Archie. "You go downstairs an' get us more whisky, all right?" He gave her a silver dollar. "This is for you, *mamita*."

She grinned and left. "So why do I gotta think?" repeated Bearclaw, impatiently.

"Thought I'd take a look at our shovels while I was out there takin' a leak. Overheard a couple of Bond's boys talkin'. I know where Carson is."

"Where's the bastard? Spread-eagled out in the cactus?"

"Just about. He's tied up pretty good. Those Mexicans know how. He ain't in very good condition. Seems he ain't gonna last long."

"Best news I've heard since Abe Lincoln was kilt! Have a drink."

"It was Mr. Bond who fixed it all."

"Hope Carson roasts in hell on a gridiron made of Yankee skeletons! A toast to Bond!"

"I also saw somethin' else," went on Archie, relentlessly.

"Ain't you the little gossiper tonight!" said Bearclaw. "Where the hell did that gal go?" He stood and walked to the edge of the staircase. Archie caught his elbow.

"Our wagon's gettin' emptied," he said.

"Our wagon's empty, we'll worry 'bout that in the mornin'. Señorita! *Venga!*"

"It's also King Fisher's wagon. And he ain't gonna like this at all. At all."

Bearclaw finally realized the implications. "You mean Bond ain't such a great guy? Is that what you mean?"

"That's what I mean."

Bearclaw leaned against the wall, and put his hand on his gun butt. "We better get goin'," he said.

"Hold it!"

"Why hold it?" yelled Bearclaw. "King Fisher'll pull our guts out and wrap 'em around a stepladder when we tell 'im!"

"That's why we gotta hold it, you goddam fool!"

Bond put his head in the room. "Any trouble, boys?" he asked.

"Nope," said Archie. "He's just tellin' me a story an' he likes to act it out. Now you sit down, Bearclaw, yo're actin' up too much."

"A good story?"

"I like it."

"Like to see you boys havin' fun. Where's the girl?"

"She went out to get us some more whisky."

"You want another one, just say the word. I want you boys to have yourselves a good time. You had a hard trip down here." He withdrew.

"I'm tellin' you he's smart," said Archie quietly. "You better talk quiet, too, or you really will get your guts wound around a stepladder. You gonna lissen?"

"Go on."

"You ain't gonna scare Bond with that. The only way you and me are gonna come out of this without King Fisher usin' that stepladder while he tells us we just came out of a good girls' school back East is to get someone really smart around here to run things."

"You crazy, you little snot-nosed kid—"

"Because," Archie went on patiently, "there's only one guy who can finish the deal O.K. You know who. An' King Fisher likes him too. When King Fisher finds out we had a chance to save Carson's ass, and we didn't try—man, we better start headin' south an' not stop till we get to Guatemala. You ready to ask Bond for a cut out of the deal and ride for Guatemala City?"

Bearclaw was silent.

"Well?" asked Archie.

"You know I got a wife and two kids," muttered Bearclaw.

Archie stood up and waited.

"I don't like to agree with you. Goddammit! Goddam you, you little needle-nosed punk, how we gonna find 'im in the dark?" The girl came back in with a bottle and set it down on the table. Her skirt was still wet. She took the lantern off the wall hook, set it on the table, and began drying her skirt by holding it over the lantern.

"Nice legs, huh?" said Bearclaw.

"Tell her you're gonna take a leak." Bearclaw pantomimed he was going to take a leak, she nodded, heedless, and the two men walked out, sobering rapidly.

They neared the stable quietly. Two men were handing out cases to a third, who was stacking them. Bond was leaning against a wall, under a lantern, smoking a cigar and checking off the cases on a sheet of paper.

"Put 'em up," said Archie. "Better hurry up," he added. "I'm drunk an' I might squeeze this here hair trigger an' not mean it. Against the wall. Bearclaw, pull out their guns. You better not try to use him to cover yourselves and try for a shot at me, neither."

"Look here," said Bond. "You men are just cuttin' yourselves a nice big hunk of trouble. And after I treated you so good."

Bearclaw threw their guns under the wagon seat. "Mr. Bond," he said thickly, "I'm dumb an' I know it." He held on to the side of the wagon for support. "But I don' like to be treated like I'm dumb. You know what I mean?" he went on, anxiously. "It makes me feel like I'm really dumb. It gets me mad," he added, becoming red with annoyance and waving his Colt muzzle back and forth.

The four men against the wall stared at the muzzle as if they were paralyzed.

"So shut up!" Bearclaw bellowed.

"They're shut up," said Archie. "For crissakes stop yellin'!"

"O.K.," said Bearclaw, mollified. He leaned against the wagon and belched. He closed his eyes. After a second he opened them again. "What we come in for?" he demanded of Archie. "We musta come in here for somethin'."

"To get our guns back," said Archie patiently.

"O.K.," said Bearclaw efficiently. "Who's stupid? I ain't stupid. I mean I'm stupid but not as stupid as you guys think. First thing I want you to do—what's the first thing they gotta do, Archie?"

"Oh, jeez," muttered Archie. "Man, you *are* stupid. Bearclaw, move back. Mr. Bond, why don't you an' your men there load up again?"

Archie sat on a bale of straw and watched. In ten minutes the wagon was full again.

"Hitch up the team," said Archie, "saddle up our two horses, an' we're gonna rent one of your saddle horses. An' rent a saddle."

"You're stealin' them," said Bond. "I got witnesses. You'll hang."

"No, we ain't," said Archie. "My uncle will pay. Now all you guys lie down on your bellies."

"Do me a favor," said Archie, "put your Colt away. I don't want it goin' off in my ear on this lousy road."

"Think they'll stay tied up long?" asked Bearclaw, shoving his Colt in the holster.

"They'll work loose by sunup."

"What we gonna do next?"

"We better hide this goddam wagon and get someone smart. When the sun is up they'll be all over like fleas on a Mex dog."

"They're gonna find us too!"

"Aw, shut up. This here road's sandy. It won't show wheel tracks much. We'll cut off somewheres and hide it in the chaparral. They'll think we went screechin' back to King Fisher and they'll keep on goin'. Keep your eyes peeled for a nice little cut-off."

They found one in the next five minutes. They swung off, Archie got down and smoothed out the wheel and hoof marks they had made turning in, and ten minutes later he pulled the wagon into some thick underbrush. He stuck several branches into the opening from the trail, smoothed the wagon tracks away.

"That'll hold," he said satisfied. He threw the spare saddle over the spare horse, and mounting, turned to Bearclaw.

"Ready?" he asked.

"Yeah. Ready," said Bearclaw. "Ready and not willin'."

Chapter Thirteen

Carson thought he was going to die. He had been hanging in the same position all night, and as dawn approached it became chilly. The numbness had crept along his arms and legs until he had the peculiar sensation of possessing a living head on a dead body, but from time to time feeling returned in an agonizing manner.

Breathing was painful in his position; the extreme retraction of his upper arms had tightened his chest muscles, and it was very difficult to expand his lungs against that savage pressure.

He began to shiver uncontrollably. He wore nothing but a thin, torn shirt and a pair of jeans. His guard had wrapped himself in a wool serape and was huddled close to his tiny fire. The fire was too far away for even the faintest glimmer of warmth to reach Carson. From time to time the guard had gotten up, felt Carson's bonds, and satisfied, had sat down again and re-wrapped himself in his serape.

Two large hands went around the guard's neck. When he had stopped struggling, part of his shirt was ripped off, shoved in his mouth, and the sleeve ripped off and used to hold the gag in place. Then his arms and legs were tied. It was efficiently done and Carson stared, but in the darkness he could see very little. The guard was sat up, the serape placed around him, the sombrero placed on his head, and to the casual passerby he looked as if he might still be on watch.

Carson felt two arms go around his waist. At the same time the riata holding his arms in the air was cut. His body sagged but two strong arms held him. A knife flashed twice and his legs were free. He could not stand and when the two men put his arms around their shoulders he almost screamed with the pain in the already viciously stretched tendons.

One of the men whispered, "The son-of-a-bitch can't walk."

73

"I know he can't walk, you dumb bastard," hissed the other. "What worries me is the way they strung 'im up all night. Can he hold the goddam reins? That's what worries me. Because when the Mexes find out, we better be makin' good time. They'll be maddern' a wet grizzly and maybe no river will stop 'em."

They were silent till they reached their horses, a quarter of a mile away. One was a grey. On her right flank was her brand; against the light color the dark brand stood out: KF.

"Archie?" asked Carson, unbelieving.

"Shut up," hissed Archie. He boosted Carson into the saddle.

"Can you ride?" he whispered venomously.

"Don't think so. Can't close my hands."

Archie cursed for a moment.

"Aincha got no more sense than that?" mumbled Bearclaw under his breath. "You'll have them *bandidos* down on us with all that bellyachin'."

"For crissakes," said Archie, "the son-of-a-bitch is gonna fall off an' they're gonna pick us off like ripe berries off a bush. Jesus, we tried. Let's shove off while we still got a chance."

"He coulda rotted on that log back there like a mushroom for all I care but we gotta bring 'im back. Help me instead of cryin' like a baby." He boosted Carson onto the saddle on his stomach and then threw one of Carson's legs viciously over the horn. The strain on his already stretched tendons was more than he could bear. He let out an involuntary moan.

"Stop your yellin'," said Archie. "I knew you was yella."

Carson lay his face against the horse's neck. It was the only way he could keep from fainting. In his exhaustion and agony he had the persistent wish that he might have taken the girl with him who had taken his heel out of the stirrup when he hung there helplessly.

He bit his thumb to keep from moaning when he felt Bearclaw lashing his legs together under his horse's belly.

A wind blew from the general's remuda toward their three horses. Carson's horse lifted his head, sniffed the air, and smelled the mares. He whinnied. Two of the mares whinnied in answer.

"Holy Christ!" said Archie, and slapped the horse on his nose.

"Leave my horse alone!" said Bearclaw.

"He'll get us kilt!" gritted Archie, almost in a wail. "Tie him on good and let's move!"

Shouts came from the direction of the camp.

"Help me, you little squirt!"

The two of them pressed Carson forward till he lay flat against the horse's neck. They lashed him to the saddle horn. Some of the loops went across his spine where he had been gouged by the spikes. He bit his lips once more to prevent any sound of agony.

They trotted out from the underbrush into the trail. Enough light now came from the east for Carson to see them clearly. Both were unshaven and to Carson they both looked as if there were other places they had much rather be. They returned Carson's stare with irritation.

The sun was a huge red ball half over the horizon and sliding up quickly.

"Man, let's *go*," said Archie fervently. He went first, holding the reins of Carson's horse, and broke into a fast trot, and, then hearing the yells from the rear, broke into a gallop. Bearclaw followed, his carbine out. The three horses pounded hard toward the Rio Grande, four miles away. The noise from the rear became clearer—they could now hear hoof beats.

Carson knew that his dead weight against the neck was slowing his horse. Archie kept cursing and pulling hard on the reins, as if he believed that would make Carson's horse go faster, and Bearclaw slashed its hindquarters with his doubled-up riata. The sound of hooves to the rear got closer. By the end of fifteen minutes the horses were lathered with foam and slowing down, but they were only three hundred yards from the river. The Mexicans had moved up so that they were the same distance behind.

The sun's lower edge had cleared the horizon. Bearclaw's horse suddenly began bucking. It had been shot in the left buttock. He sawed desperately at the reins and managed to force it towards the river, firing several shots to his rear. The shots made their pursuers scatter from the trail, but the horse, crazed with pain, began plunging sidewards and suddenly stumbled. Bearclaw landed on all fours.

They could hear the shrill ululation of triumph from the Mexicans.

But they had only a hundred feet to go. Bearclaw caught

hold of Archie's stirrup and was pulled in great leaps. The horses plunged in at a run and began swimming. The current carried them downstream, but the horses were swimming strongly. Three-quarters of the way across the first Mexican appeared.

They did not have enough sense to dismount and fire prone, Carson saw, and they kept firing from the nervous, shifting platforms of their panting horses. More arrived and began firing.

In a minute the Texans' horses felt ground under their feet. They plunged up the gently sloping bank. The firing stopped.

Carson heard the familiar voice call across the river. "*Oye, Tejano!*" it called. Archie untied Carson. He sat up.

Across the river the general sat his horse, one hand on a hip, the other holding the butt of his carbine on his thigh. Carson was dizzy and nauseous; he held on to the horn with both hands. He turned and faced Mexico.

"*Que quieres?*" he asked.

The general beckoned him to Mexico with a sweep of his hand. "*Al frente, amigo,*" he called. "*Vamos hablar un poquito. Estamos amigos, Tejano!*"

Carson shook his head, too weak and too sick to trust himself to speak.

"*No?*" asked the general. "*Que lástima!*"

He turned to his men and told them that the Texan was rejecting their hospitality. They roared. He turned again and faced Carson.

"*Adios!*" he called out.

"Tell him it's not *adios,* tell him it's *hasta la vista,*" whispered Carson.

"Tell 'im yourself," said Archie.

Carson straightened up, even though the effort was agonizing. He knew his voice would not carry across the river. Everything was swimming in a red haze. He was not sure which of the blurred figures was the general.

He lifted the middle finger of his right hand in a gesture of obscene derision.

The general roared with laughter, took off his sombrero, bowed with exaggerated politeness, and waved his sombrero towards Mexico. The men around him melted into the chaparral.

Chapter Fourteen

Carson woke up again. He had been fainting and waking and fainting and waking again. He realized that he was not tied to a horse any more—he also realized, in a vague way, that he was not thirsty any more, but then he dropped off to unconsciousness again without knowing that an old Mexican woman had been placing a water-soaked rag in the corner of his mouth.

Once more he came to. He was lying on his stomach on a mattress made of burlap stuffed with corn shucks. It was late in the afternoon. He was naked. The old woman was placing something cool, wet and soothing on his wrenched shoulders and his lower back. His left eye still throbbed painfully, although the red haze had almost completely disappeared.

"You feel all right?" a voice asked.

Carson started to roll to the left to look at his questioner. His spine stabbed with agony.

"Better," he said, staring at the big mass in the dim adobe hut.

"Yeah, I'll bet," said Bearclaw. "Every time I started to talk to you so far you fainted. If you're gonna do it again, tell me now. I don' wanna waste my breath."

"I feel fine," said Carson.

"All right. Lemme tell you right now. We came across the river for one reason—we'd catch hell from King Fisher if we didn't. For my part I don't give a damn what they did to you. You probably deserved. Archie feels the same way, doncha, Archie?"

Archie grunted assent. Carson said nothing.

"We figger," said Bearclaw brusquely, "that if Bond fixed a foxy grandpaw like you he could go to town all over us. And we'd never know what hit us till it was all over and by

83

then ol' King Fisher would be sittin' on top of a barrel of rattlers with us inside."

"Where are we?"

"Dunno. We took one look at you when we untied you an' we just stopped the first place we saw. We tol' 'em you was knocked unconscious by a low branch in the dark an' then your horse dragged you. An' then we found you."

Carson held up his swollen wrists. "How'd you explain these?"

"She didn't ask, we ain't tellin', an' we told her we'd pay her plenty. Here comes her old man now."

An old Mexican was tying his burro to the branch of the cottonwood outside. He eyed them shrewdly.

"We sent him to town for medicine," said Bearclaw.

"How do you know he won't talk?"

"We don't know," said Archie. "But we're lucky. That general crossed over here last year and killed all his goats and barbecued them an' shot his nephew for tryin' to collect. I told him we're here to fight the general an' he's our friend. Besides we're on top of a little ridge here, the old guy's sheep got the ground clipped close like a billiard table so no one kin creep up on us too easy."

Carson nodded approvingly, and watched the old woman prepare the salve her husband had bought.

"What do we do next?" Archie asked.

"We sit her a day or two till I can move. In the meantime we find out what's on everyone's mind." He turned to the old man.

"What's your name, señor?"

"Sebastiano Valdes, *a sus órdenes*," said the old man, bowing.

"Tomás Carson," said Carson, bowing from his prone position by nodding his head. The old man smiled, pleased.

"Archie, get me my saddlebags," Carson asked. Archie got them without complaint. Carson took out a twenty dollar gold piece. He gave it to the old man, who held it with awe in his dark calloused palm. Probably, Carson thought, it was the first one he had ever owned. He took out two more, showed them to old Valdes, and replaced them. "One for today," he said, "one for each day we'll stay here—"

"Sixty bucks!" said Bearclaw, aggrieved. "That's as much as I get a month!"

"He's gonna earn his," said Carson. Archie tittered.

Carson said he would pay well for accurate information on certain topics. If the information he received was not correct, he, unlike the general, did not have to cross the river to show his disappointment. Old Valdes sat with his gnarled brown hands in his lap. He nodded calmly.

"First," began Carson, "where is Bond? Second, when I was a guest at the general's I heard someone say something about a Federal army on its way up from Chihuahua to deal with him. Where is it? And the third—you will give this note to the general—"

Valdes shrugged, smiling.

"What's the matter?"

"He can not read. He will have to give it to someone to read for him. There will be a priest, maybe—he will not trust the priest. So—" Valdes shrugged.

Carson slowly tore up the note.

"But he knows me," said Valdes. "I will tell him."

Carson told him what he wanted the general to know. The old man rose, said *"Bueno,"* and disappeared.

"What you gonna do now?" asked Bearclaw, nervously.

"You're gonna get the old lady all the water and firewood she wants. Then you're gonna sit on that hill with Archie an' fire a couple warning shots anyone get too close."

"Yeah," went on Bearclaw, "but what you gonna do?"

"Sleep," said Carson.

At nine that night Valdes stepped behind Archie on the ridge and coughed politely. Archie hurled himself sidewards in desperate haste and worked the lever of his carbine as he skinned the left side of his face on the rough ground.

"Estoy yo!" shouted the old man. *"Amigo, amigo!"*

"Goddamit!" said Archie, getting up and holding his scratched face, "you almost got kilt, sneaking up on me like that."

The old man did not explain that he very frequently did not approach his house by the trail. Ambush was too easy along the border, there were too many enemies. He came over the ridge, saw Archie, and decided to cough as a well-bred way of attracting his attention.

Valdes' wife shook Carson awake. He felt much better. He found he could sit up without much pain. He sat on the old mattress with his back against the cool adobe bricks, and lit a cigarette. The old man rolled a cigarette. Bearclaw leaned against the wall and watched.

"Were you followed?"

"No."

"Good. And Bond?"

"Señor Bond looked for your wagon toward King Fisher's ranch for fifty miles. He then came back to Isleta and sent a telegram to King Fisher. It said you were dead, that your two men had refused his offer of help, and that unless he sent the wagon back with someone more intelligent the whole arrangement would be useless."

"How—" began Carson. The old man went on, "My niece's husband's son sweeps the telegraph office. He has trained himself to read Morse. The Texan there does not know this."

"Very good. Next?"

"I went to Saragoza to sell some chile peppers and to visit my cousin Hilario who works in the only hotel. He is a good boy, he listens to everyone. The army is marching from Chihuahua. They have artillery. They have many good officers, trained in France. They will have about five thousand troops. Another army is coming from Monterey. They will squeeze the general. It is said they have orders to take no prisoners."

Carson grinned. "And the third?"

"The general will meet you where you say."

"*Muchas gracias.*"

"*Por nada.*"

"What's he say?" asked Bearclaw, rising up on one elbow.

"Tomorrow at noon," said Carson, looking at the ceiling and smiling, "I meet the general on San Vicente Island."

"What's San Vicente?"

"It's an island smack in the middle of the Rio Grande. It ain't Mexico and it ain't Texas. Very neutral."

"You don't look neutral."

"I ain't. I don't feel neutral. We got a problem, though. The general's gonna want them carbines for nothin'. He needs 'em very bad, very bad. He ain't gonna care much how he gets 'em or who he hurts gettin' 'em. We will have to be very neutral and very smart tomorrow."

"How many men does he have?"

Carson turned to Valdes. The old man looked up from his cold tortillas. "Mebbe tousand, mebbe twelve hondred," he said.

"He gonna bring 'em all to the island?"

"Not enough room. He's gonna leave the men and the cattle in Mexico and he comes alone to the island. I leave my army in Texas an' I go alone to meet 'im. He has his men bring over, say, thirty head from Mexico. I give him one carbine and a hundred rounds. He brings over another thirty head. I give him another carbine and one hundred more rounds. That way I don't get burned bad if somethin' goes wrong. An' he don't either."

"It don't sound so good to me."

Carson lifted an eyebrow. "You got a better idea?"

Bearclaw was silent. He chewed his tortilla a moment. "What I don't see," he said, "is how we're gonna persuade him we're an army. When he sees there's just three of us with all those nice new Winchesters sitting in them crates, what's gonna stop him from rushing us? That dotted line in the middle of the river? I don't like it. I don't see why I gotta put my neck right in that rope, no sirree."

"I agree," said Carson. "No reason for him not to take all the stuff an' not pay for it. He's got a good reason to do it—if he don't get them carbines, he don't care if he makes King Fisher mad. But there's one reason why he ain't gonna make the rush."

"You're sure, eh, Carson? I ain't."

"I am. We got an army."

"You got fever?"

"The old man and his two nephews and his two grandsons are gonna herd the stock and hold it once it's on Texas. You two are gonna look like an army."

"Looka here, Carson, I don't have to go along with you this far. I jus' wanna tell you—"

"We'll leave at sunup. We got lots to do before the general arrives on his side of the river."

"Yeah, but—"

"*Hasta la mañana.* I need sleep." He turned over and pulled up his blanket. Bearclaw stood up, looked at the old man, rotated his forefinger in the air over his right ear several times, and pointed at Carson. The old man smiled and moved his forefinger slowly back and forth in the negative sign of Mexico.

"Oh no, Señor," he said, "oh no."

Chapter Fifteen

San Vicente was a low sand bar one hundred and fifty feet long; at its widest it was fifty feet. It tapered to a sandy point at both ends. On the upstream end driftwood had piled up in a tangle of branches bleached white by the furious sun till they were the color of old bones. Low-growing shrubs grew in scattered clumps over the island. The Mexican side had a wide mud shore, cracked in flat slabs by the sun; back of the shore ocotillo and willow and cottonwood grew thickly so that hundreds of men could hide in it totally unobserved from the Texan side. The same impenetrability was true of the other shore; only a hundred feet back from the shore was a small hill covered with dense shrubbery to its top.

Just after sunup the wagon with its load of carbines and ammunition creaked to a halt. Valdes and his nephews and grandsons reined in. Carson ordered Archie and Bearclaw to break open three cases. They did so, puzzled; Carson had not yet told them of his plans. As they were opening the crates he slowly and painfully got down from his seat on the wagon. Valdes dragged Carson's saddle from the wagon and saddled his horse.

Grimacing with pain, Carson mounted.

The crates were open.

"All right," Carson said. "You got thirty. Load 'em."

Still puzzled, the men loaded the carbines.

Carson turned to Valdes. He told the old man to scout the other side of the river, to see if anyone were there and watching, to come on back as soon as he had made sure. He was to keep his men scouting the area, however.

The old man nodded and took his vaqueros into the river.

Carson turned. "You two spread out and scatter the carbines behind bushes and in the forks of trees, anywhere it looks like a natural place to cover me when I'm on the island. Point 'em all towards me. I'll be in the middle of the island, so aim 'em that way. If I move a little follow me with a couple. When that's done, Archie, you go on up to the hill with your Springfield. Find a good place. Take plenty of water, an' a bite to eat. Make yourself plenty of shade. You're not gonna leave that place or move, mebbe till late afternoon. I wanna be covered all that time. Every second." He paused, and looked at Archie's face. "Like the idea of me in your sights?" Archie said nothing, but it was obvious to Carson that he liked the idea very much.

"You're pretty good, your uncle says. Show me."

"Show you what?"

Carson pulled a silver dollar out of his pocket. "When you see this dollar go all the way up in the air I want it knocked spinnin'."

"You want the edge nicked or you want it hit dead center?"

"Dead center is fine."

Archie took his Springfield from under the seat. "How about a little bet?" he asked.

"All right. Five bucks says you won't dead center."

"You got a bet, Carson."

"You're gonna have to watch me pretty close all the time I'm there talkin'. An' not take your eyes off me for a second."

"I'll watch you like you was a rabbit an' I was a hungry rattler."

"I'll bet," said Carson dryly. "First you an' Bearclaw an' Valdes set up the carbines so they look good to me out there."

"To the general too, huh?"

"To the general especially."

Carson rode out to the island. Valdes rode out of the thicket and called out that no one had been there all night and that no one was in sight. Carson told him to keep scouting and let him know as soon as a stranger came into the area.

In an hour the carbines were set up. Carson corrected several positions. He called Bearclaw over to the island.

"Looks pretty good," Carson said. "When they get here, you and Valdes move from one to another. Sort of move the muzzles a bit, as if someone is covering me every time I move. Move them whenever the general or one of his men moves around. Once in a while let 'em see a shirt or a hat. Cover a lot of ground. Move one way at the right. Then one in the middle, one near the right, then back to the left—you get it?"

"I gotta hand it to you, Carson," Bearclaw said grudgingly. He rode back while Carson sat in the shade of his horse drawing brands in the sand with a twig.

The sun was about to touch the zenith when Valdes trotted into the river, followed by his relatives. The young men were looking over their shoulders in an excited manner.

"They're almost here," said Valdes. "Many, many!"

Carson told him what to do with the carbines. "*Si*," said the old man, grinning. Carson told them not to act surprised if a shot should come from the hill above them; that they should act as if shooting like that were common. They were to appear confident and serene, as if hundreds of men were backing them up.

"Think you can do it?" Carson asked.

"They will do it," promised Valdes, grimly. "I brought them up to show respect to a man who deserves it." He turned to the young men and asked, "Do you understand what the patrón says?" They nodded. "Good," said Valdes. "Is anyone scared?" No one spoke. "Good," he repeated. "We are ready."

Almost immediately the general appeared on the shore. Several men followed and spread out on either side. They carefully scanned the other side. But the general was the first to catch sight of the carbine barrels. He turned and spoke sharply. Two men trotted to the rear and disappeared into the thicket.

Carson stood up, painfully. The general took off his sombrero and bowed ironically. Carson nodded. The general replaced his sombrero, grinned, and spoke something to Pablo, who laughed, holding his hand over his mouth. The two of them rode into the river.

They looked down at Carson, who began to unstrap the bedroll from the cantle.

"Not nice, *amigo*," said the general reprovingly, jerking his head at the carbine barrels protruding from tree forks and from bushes.

"I learn as I go along," said Carson, patting the blanket beside him.

"No, no, I don' like it." The general still sat his horse, frowning down at Carson.

"You have me covered too. I'm not complainin'. Set."

"All right, *Tejano*," the general said with a sudden grin. "I get off. We talk bus'ness." He dismounted and gave the reins to Pablo. Up to now Carson had not been able to get a good look at the man, since his face was in shadow. Now he saw that Pablo had a patch over one eye and that several of his front teeth had jagged edges; his nose was swollen and the area under his eyes was black and blue. Pablo took the reins, scowling down at Carson. Carson calmly went on drawing cattle brands in the sand.

The general squatted on his haunches close to Carson. "You are lookin' good," he said critically. "Well, per'aps not so good. But better than the last time I saw you, no?" Carson said nothing. The general picked up a twig and began drawing in the sand as he talked. "You surprise me," he went on. "I don' think you would get to Texas, I don' think you live till morning. Fonny," he went on, amused, "there is Texas, back there is Mexico. One hundred feet, you kill me, one hundred feet that way I kill you. Here we are friends. Fonny. No?"

"Fonny," said Carson.

"You make fon of me?"

"My back hurts, general. I still don't see so good. I don't like you, general. You rub me a little bit too much the wrong way an' I just might take you with me up shit creek. Suppose we get down to business right away. It's hot here an' I'm gettin' thirsty."

The general said nothing for a minute. His face was hidden under his sombrero rim as he stared at the ground and the patterns he was making with his twig. "You lucky," he said, finally. "You lucky you got all those men there, Carson. All right, we talk business! One more question I wanna ask you."

"Go ahead."

"How you feel when you get to Texas, eh?"

"Wet clothes in Texas are a damn sight more comfortable than dry ones in Mexico," said Carson.

"Hey, tha's good!" shouted the general. "*Oye, Pablito, ven acá!*"

Pablo shambled over, staring down at Carson with hatred. The general translated Carson's remark. Pablo said nothing.

"Trouble with Pablo," said the general impatiently, turning back to Carson, "is that ever since he lost his eye he thinks nothin' is fonny. He——"

Pablo tugged the general's sleeve and whispered in his ear. The general's look of irritation vanished. A thoughtful look swept over his face. He turned to Carson.

"Pablo thinks very fonny," he said. "He thinks maybe you don' have so many men there." Carson looked at Pablo.

He forced himself to smile calmly. Pablo was staring at him very closely.

"*Porque*?" Carson asked, idly.

"Where would you get so many men so soon?" Pablo asked in Spanish, and shrugged.

"You think I'm bluffing?" Pablo shrugged again, more elaborately, and smiled, covering his broken teeth with a large dirty hand. Carson took a silver dollar from his pocket. He gave it to Pablo.

"It's yours," Carson said. "All you have to do is hold it high, all the way, for five seconds."

Pablo stared at him suspiciously.

"Afraid?" asked Carson. Pablo grabbed the dollar and held his arm high, staring at Carson. Carson smiled but he was praying inside.

Two seconds later the coin leaped out of Pablo's hand as if it were alive and spun away in a silver blur. While it was still spinning there followed the harsh blast of the explosion. The general snapped his head around and stared at the hill. A tiny smoke puff drifted up slowly. Then he picked up the silver dollar. Dead center. The general looked again at the Texas shore. Two of the carbines shifted a little. There was a flash of a shirt behind a tree fork.

"Hey, *Tejano*," said the general thoughtfully, "you wanna work for me?" He looked again at the dollar. "Bring him, too," he added, pointing to the hill. Carson shook his head.

"We have a good time, we move around a lot. We drink plenty pulque, maybe for you we get weesky, we take plenty of Nañita's cattle——"

"Whose?"

"Nañita, Nañita! Grandmother. That's what we call all the cattle in Texas. You don' know this word? No? You *Tejanos* stole Texas, no? All that cattle over there——" here he waved his hand casually all along the Texas shore—"all that cattle is Nañita's. We just come to take it back. Well, we sell them to rich hacenderos in Sonora, Neuvo Leon, nobody very particular down there about 'merican brands. Or maybe we sell 'em in Arizona, maybe New Mexico. Nobody care too much except maybe Cattlemen's Association inspectors, but how many men they got? So. We take the money, we put it in a bank in Francia, Italia. Three, four years from now we go to Paris, eh? We be very rich, *Tejano!* You smart, you got *cojones*. Pablo ain't so smart an' he ain't good no more, I gotta get rid of him."

"No."

"I make you a general too."

"No."

"You like that Luisa de Parral?"

Carson kept his face expressionless.

"You come with me as general, you can have her."

Carson felt his heart leap like a trout after a well-cast fly. He thought this must be a careful trap; he would have to watch his way here very carefully, he knew. He shook his head slightly.

"No? I thought you like this one. Nobody touch her yet. Maybe me, a little. She fight, she fight!"

"No," said Carson. He had a very good card to play, but it could wait.

"You wan' to get to business? You *norte americanos,* all the time business, business! All right. I'm a good businessman. We start. First thing. I give good stock, no culls. You send one carbine, one hundred cartridges to Mexico, I send across twenty head. You—"

"Twenty-five."

"Carson, I make arrangements with King Fisher before I even know you live. Twenty cattle—"

"Twenty-five."

The general looked down at the sand. He drew a circle with his twig and stabbed the little piece of wood deep down into the center of the circle. Without looking up he said slowly, "I don' like this much."

"Me neither. Twenty-five."

"No good to get mad. Me or you. Too hot. Too many people around here with guns, no? Twenty."

"Twenty-five."

The general rose. "You make jokes, *amigo.*" He put a foot in his stirrup. "This heat makes you crazy. If I dont' take your guns all you got is scrap iron."

"You gotta come back to me," said Carson softly, "an' you know it."

"Why, *Tejano*?" The general swung a greasy leg over the saddle and settled back.

"I bet you play poker pretty good."

"Pretty good. Maybe we play later."

"We're playin' now. You're bluffin' an' I got all the cards. Set down again."

"I don' like this talk. Say what you mean."

"In three days, maybe four, you're gonna have to fight the Mex army. You're not gonna do too well. Each man of yours who's got a carbine—and that's one out of ten—has only got three or four rounds left."

"You keep your ears open, eh?"

"I keep 'em open."

"All right. You know. All right, I need them bad. Twenty-five."

"Not any more."

"What you mean? Maybe I don' understand your English. May—"

"You understand all right. Since we been arguin' about price I been gettin' thirsty. Every time I get thirsty the price goes up. The price is now thirty."

The general looked at Carson. His hands twisted the reins so tightly the knuckles were pale. Finally he spoke. "Some day we meet again. Maybe in hell, *Tejano*, it don' matter. I wait for you. Eh?"

"I had a day and a night to think about you, general. You're gettin' off easy. If I was really mad I'd break them carbines right in front of you an' watch you go crazy. But I'm nice. Because I'm gonna let you fight that Mex army with guns and ammunition."

"All right. I don' wanna talk no more. Thirty head, one carbine."

"And two more things I want."

"Well?"

"I want my horse back."

"All ri'."

"A good saddle to replace the one you ruined."

"All ri'. How's your back?"

Carson ignored the remark. He added, "And Luisa de Parral."

The general leaned back in his saddle and smiled. Then he

turned and spoke quietly to Pablo. Pablo's mouth dropped open in amazement. He looked incredulous. The general repeated his orders. Pablo grinned and stared at Carson and rode into the river. The general said, "*Amigo*, if I have no army to fight now, you know what I do?"

"Sure, you'd finish where you left off with that brandin' iron."

"You're damn right."

"If I didn't have you in my sniper's sights. You forget that."

"Hey, listen, *Tejano*, no kiddin', you come with me. I make you a general, jus' like me, eh? You bring your man with you, the one who shoot so good."

Carson grinned and stood up. He faced the Texas shore and yelled, "One case carbines, one case ammo!"

Valdes and one of his nephews brought them across to the island. The old man took a small crowbar and pried one case open. The general smiled as he took out one carbine. It was heavily smeared with grease. He worked the lever action lovingly. He set it down again, wiped his hands on his charro trousers and held up both hands, facing the Mexican shore. His fingers outstretched, he closed both hands. He repeated this three times. Several men on horseback nodded and rode into the bushes. Five minutes later they came out with thirty head. As they passed the island on their way to the other shore Carson scrutinized them carefully. He rejected two. The general whistled sharply and held up two fingers. Two more cattle were driven into the river. Valdes' nephews and grandsons met them in the middle of the river and swam them to Texas.

The general said, staring at the Valdes men, "I think I know where you get your information, *amigo*." Carson did not answer.

Carson sat on his blanket and stared at the little herd that was now held against the hill. King Fisher had told him to ask for twenty head for each carbine. He was now getting thirty. The extra ten were his, he considered—and if the rest of the trading went well, if he could get away with the cattle, and then find a buyer—he would soon be a wealthy man. He knew he might have trouble with King Fisher about the extra cattle, and to whom they belonged. He would risk that. He would have trouble with lots of people about those cattle—the Cattlemen's Association inspectors, who would like to know how he had possession of so many stolen brands, Mr. Bond, Comanches or Apaches who considered passing cattle theirs since the buffalo were gone, ranchers who would object to his cattle drinking their water or who feared they might be carrying the Texas tick. He ran the risk of stampedes, where an hour's run would burn ten pounds off each head, quicksand, locoweed.

The afternoon wore on. When it became too dark to examine the cattle with accuracy the Mexicans withdrew, and Carson splashed across to the Texas side. After a restless, wary night he rode again to the island and began again the weary job of tallying. By the time Luisa appeared on his horse on the southern bank, most of the cattle had been crossed. Both of her hands rested on the pommel of the saddle the general was giving Carson in exchange. Pablo led the horse by the reins. She rode astride; when her horse came out of the river the water cascaded down her bare legs.

There was a fresh bruise on her cheek; Pablo's face had now acquired several scratches. They were still bleeding. He noticed Carson's curious stare and grinning, he wiped his sleeve across them. By now she was close enough for Carson to see that her wrists were tied to the pommel.

"She don' wan' to come, *Tejano*," said the general. "Maybe she don' like you. *Pablo, la señorita prefiría permanecer con nosotros?* Would the lady prefer staying with us?"

Pablo giggled, hiding his mouth.

"*Si, si, no quiso venir acá!* She didn't want to come here!"

Carson reached out and cut her loose. She rubbed her wrists, staring at Pablo and the general. She looked at the boxes of carbines being opened and counted.

"Am I being traded for guns?" she asked.

"Not exactly," said Carson. "You're more a kind of condition, put it that way."

"Are you helping this—this animal—fight against Mexico?"

At the word "animal" the general flushed. His hand went to his quirt, but Pablo's touch on his elbow stopped him. He swerved his glance. Carson's hand was resting lightly on his Colt butt.

"You got all the cattle now?" he said, turning his back on her.

"I got what I want," said Carson. "No reason for you to hang 'round here any more." The general nodded.

"*Momentito, mi general,*" she said with sarcasm.

The general deliberately kept his back turned to her.

"*Vamos*, Pablo," he said.

"The reason," she began, coldly and slowly in her perfect Spanish, "why people like you have been beaten by we Parrals and why your women taken by the men of my family whenever they were wanted, is because you are vermin."

She had not raised her voice, but the general jerked his reins hard and stopped in the river. She went on. "Since you are animals you must be treated like sheep or pigs or snakes. Some day I will put my heel at your throat and kill you."

The general stared at her. "*Adios, puta,*" he said, and spit in the river. He turned his horse once more to face Mexico. She reached out quickly and pulled Carson's Colt from its holster. She had the hammer back before Carson could knock her arm upward. The blast burned his face, but the bullet screamed harmlessly upwards. Before she could fire again Carson had wrenched the Colt from her, but in that moment the general had spun and lashed at her face with his quirt. Carson very carefully and very quickly hit the general on his face in exactly the same place with the barrel of his Colt. It laid the flesh open to the bone. Then he jammed the barrel three inches deep into the general's stomach. The man doubled over, gasping, his bleeding face touching the pommel. Carson covered Pablo with his gun. Pablo's hand had gone for his machete, had lifted it high, but the bullet from Archie's Springfield smashed his wrist. He screamed and dropped the machete and clasped his broken bones with his left hand.

"*Muy buenas tardes,*" said Carson dryly, and he waved them with his Colt into the river. The general pulled himself erect, and holding on to the pommel that was by now slippery with blood, he gasped, "I see you again some day, *Tejano*. You wait. Her too."

Carson watched them swim the river, his Colt resting on his thigh. He was thinking, that son of a bitch Archie, now I gotta be grateful to him.

Chapter Sixteen

"What's he gonna do with them thirty extra carbines we got left over?" demanded Archie. Bearclaw and Archie were sitting at the small campfire; back of them was the low squat mass that was the Valdes ranchito. The moon had risen and the wind had sprung up. Archie was cleaning his Springfield. "What's he gonna do with—"

"Aw, don't talk so loud," said Bearclaw. "He'll hear yuh."

Archie looked over his shoulder at the ranchito. "Yap, yap, yap, like an' old squaw," he said, but he lowered his voice. "How we gonna take back five thousand head? We need fifteen good hands for that. Where we gonna get 'em? Take three weeks to get 'em to the ranch. I don't aim to swaller that much dust."

"If it takes three weeks it takes three weeks, you pipsqueak. You swaller dust like the rest of us. Oughta put a bridle on your mouth, Archie."

Archie went on as if he had not heard. "An' the woman," he said. "Woman on a trail drive, never heard of such a thing. Didja?"

Bearclaw scraped up the last of his beans from the tin plate. He swallowed them. He wiped his mouth. He drank some coffee. He said, "You never trailed a herd nowheres, you punk kid. All you ever did was hang around a pool hall and try to get the girls in trouble, but they wouldn't let you come near 'em, pimple face. Now you shut up. I'm gonna sleep. You got first watch. Stay away from her, she'll claw your face to doll rags if you stick it too close to her. She'll go over that map of yours like a mountain lion goin' up a pine tree." He spread his tarpaulin, undid his blanket roll, and tucked himself in, his head almost vertical against his saddle, tilted the sombrero over his face to keep out the light from the fire, and closed his eyes.

"He's saddlin'," said Archie. "Where the hell is he goin'?"

"Ask 'im," said Bearclaw.

Archie said nothing. Carson walked again into the ranchito. As he walked by Luisa's bed, she said, "Señor Carson."

"Yes?"

"You leave me alone?"

The two black braids hung down.

"I'll be back."

She was silent. She leaned out. One braid swung back and forth. She caught it and held it still. Carson fought a desire to touch it.

"Pablo raped me this afternoon," she said. "When he came to take me to the island."

She stared at him. His heart began to thud so violently that he was sure she could hear it, that Señora Valdes, curled up in her bed in the other corner, with the tiny fire glinting off her gold earrings, could hear it.

He realized that if he hadn't insisted on her delivery as part of the deal she probably would be untouched, that in the wild headlong escape from the Federal army and its summary executions she probably would have been left behind.

"I'll see you get to New Orlins," he said, looking at the fire. His face felt hot and his hands suddenly seemed to be enormous. He didn't know what to do with them. "From there you can get a ship to Vera Cruz. Then you——"

"My fiancé is in Mexico City. He will not want me now."

"But your hacienda?"

She shrugged.

"Where do you want to go?"

She shrugged. She leaned back and stared at him. "You take me with you now?"

"Tomorrow."

"But not tonight?"

Carson took out his Colt, checked it, and gave it to her. She looked relieved as she held it.

"You come back?"

"Later."

"And you won't leave me alone here?"

"No." She smiled and settled back.

Carson got to Isleta two hours later. The saloon was half empty. Bond was nowhere in sight. Carson's horse moved on, his hoofs muffled in the thick dust. Bond lived in a frame house near his office. Carson dismounted, pulled his Winchester from the saddle scabbard, and sauntered down the street, a canvas sack over his arm. Through the half-drawn curtains he could see Bond sitting at a table under a strong kerosene light. He was eating a thick sandwich and making entries in a ledger. Back of him Carson could see the huge black mass of a locked safe. On the table lay a Colt. Bond took a bite from the sandwich, made an entry with a pen, and drank some beer.

Carson tapped quietly at the window. Bond put down the half-eaten sandwich and grabbed the Colt. He unbolted the door and peering into the darkness, asked "Who's that?"

Carson said gruffly, in Spanish, "A message from the general." He held up a folded square of paper.

"Not so loud," said Bond, nervously. "Come in." He lowered his Colt and stepped back. Carson came in. Bond bolted the door and then turning, held his hand out for the message. He looked into the muzzle of the carbine.

"Very slow," said Carson, gently, "very slow-like, gimme your Colt."

Bond's face drained white. He did as he was told.

Carson stepped back into a corner of the room so that he would not be seen from the street.

"Now pull the curtains all the way."

Bond did so.

"Take a seat, Mr. Bond." Bond sat in his chair, his fingers clutching the edge of his table so hard that his knuckles turned white.

"Finish eatin' your sandwich while I talk," said Carson. Bond picked up the sandwich, took a small bite, but he was unable to swallow.

"Throat too dry, maybe," offered Carson. He sat down opposite Bond and rested his carbine on his lap. "Drink some beer," he suggested.

As Bond's hand reached out Carson said genially, "This here thing is pointed straight at your belly. Don't get smart an' throw the bottle at me. Or don't try to turn the table over. This here carbine is cocked and has got a very light pull."

"What do you want?" asked Bond. There were a lot of grey hairs in the stubble on his unshaven face, which looked old and shrunken. Carson began to feel a little bit sorry for him.

"Aincha gonna welcome me back to Texas?" he asked.

Bond sat silently. Carson leaned forward and prodded him with the muzzle.

"Welcome back," said Bond.

"Much better," said Carson. "After my visit to Mexico, which I must admit you did your best to make pleasant, I'm gettin' used to the Mex habit of talkin' 'bout the weather and relatives before gettin' down to business. How's your wife?"

No answer came. Carson prodded him with the muzzle again.

Bond grunted as the muzzle dug into his stomach.

"Fine," he gasped.

"Your father?"

"Dead."

"Sorry to hear that. How's your sister?"

"Ain't got a sister."

"We shore could use some rain. Couldn't we?"

"Yeah."

"Good," Carson said approvingly. "You ain't 'xactly boilin' over with gossip, but that ain't bad. Now let's get down to business. I could kill you now an' get away an' no one could catch me. Or even know it was me that done it. An' you wouldn't blame me at all. Would you?"

Bond stared at him. His lips were as grey as the stubble on his face, and when Carson began to feel sorry for him he thought of the night he had spent with his arms twisted high in the air behind his back. Then he felt not sorry at all.

"Look at my eyes, Mr. Bond. Tell me what you see."

Bond licked his dry lips and leaned forward. "They look sort of red," he said.

"You know why?"

Bond shook his head.

"Your friend the general has got a great sense of humor. I ain't in a very good mood. But we can still do business. I got twenty-seven hundred head, two year olds, no scrubs. They're yours at twenty bucks a head. You want to buy 'em, doncha?" He leaned forward and prodded. "Doncha, Mr. Bond?"

Bond grunted with pain and nodded.

"Good. That's fifty-four thousand bucks. Also with 'em I'm offerin' thirty carbines. Never been fired, just had the grease wiped offa them, an' after a day's exercise we put

'em back in their crates, good as new. I'm offerin' 'em at
a hundred bucks apiece. That's a bargain too."

"One hundred! I can get all I want at forty!"

"Yeah. I know. But this is a special bargain."

"What's so special about it? I can maybe use the cattle if
they're as good as you say they are, but what the hell's so
special about carbines at a hundred?"

Carson looked at him and leaned back carefully. His back
hurt badly and he sought to find a position which afforded
him the least pain. When he had found it he spoke.

"Special," he said patiently, but with his teeth set hard,
"because they're offered by me. Call it a bonus because of
the welcome I got from your buddy, the general. I feel like
I already wasted a lot of your time, it's gettin' late an' all.
You'll be wantin' to get to bed. That'll be a grand total of
fifty-seven thousand. Since you an' I know you got it in
that safe back of you, just get it out. Thank you kindly."

Bond kneeled on the floor and turned the combination
lock. For half a minute he spun it back and forth, the
tumbler's clicking making the only sound in the room. He
pulled the big handle down, swung the big door outward,
reached in, and grabbed the Colt placed inside on the top
shelf for just such an emergency. He shielded himself behind
the safe door, spun around and lifted the Colt.

Carson was not there. Bond had not heard Carson moving
to the other side of the safe; from this new position Carson
was covering his back.

"And one makes two," Carson said cheerfully; he reached
out and took the Colt from Bond's hand. He shoved it in his
belt. "Spoils of war," he added. "Don't go 'round sayin' I
stole 'em either. Man pulls a gun on you, you got a right
to take it. An' you can sell those cattle for a nice profit up
north. Don't know why you take on so."

Bond began to count out the money.

"Sell 'em hell!" he snarled. "That's King Fisher's cattle
and he'll grab 'em!"

"No, they ain't King Fisher's cattle," said Carson. "They're
my cattle. Deal was twenty head for a carbine. I saw my
chance and got thirty. Of course, if it hadn't been for your
kind help the deal woulda gone through for twenty, but
God disposes. You're sorta tied up in this whole arrangement,
in a manner of speakin', Mr. Bond. King Fisher is gettin'
what he bargained for. You got a nice touch when you count

out greenbacks, Mr. Bond," Carson went on, admiringly. He reached out for the money, stepped back, and counted it. "Hope you don't mind my checkin' up," he said.

Bond's color had come back. "It don't pay to get me mad at you, Carson," he said, as he watched Carson sweep the money into the canvas sack he had brought with him. "It would be more smart if you just gave me back that money and rode away. We got long memories down here. Sooner or later—"

"Shut up. Sit down at the desk."

Carson's icy voice cut away at Bond's recently gained reassurance.

"Get one of your nice receipts."

Bond got it.

"If you woulda had a Colt or derringer stashed away in that desk drawer," said Carson, "I would let you shoot me. It ain't fair you gotta lose three guns in one evenin'. Go on now. Write 'Thomas Carson, Esquire—' be sure to put in that esquire—'has sold me twenty-seven hundred head of cattle, at twenty dollars, and also thirty new Winchesters, seventy-three model, at one hundred dollars.' Good, you don't have to write the total down, I understand it's too painful. Now write the date on top and put your John Hancock at the bottom. Now give it to me. No, not yet. Wave it around a bit and dry it. There, that's better, ain't it? Pick up your herd on Valdes' ranch tomorrow. You'll find the carbines there. Ride an' make the cow count with the Señora. She's smart an' she knows cattle. If the count ain't right tell her. I'll make it good. Any questions?"

"The Valdes family been a big help to you, ain't they?"

"It's rare you can find a family as nice as that. All right, one more thing. Almost forgot." He pulled a small, filthy, sweat-soaked piece of paper from a hip pocket. It had been soaked in river water once. He opened it carefully and held it up for Bond's inspection.

"Know it?"

"Looks like a piece of my stationery."

"Yep. It's an order of yours for fifty rolls bob wire."

"I don't need no barb wire."

"Mebbe you don't. But you wrote it out. So you owe me four hundred more, F.O.B. Damn fair price." Bond stubbornly refused to move. Carson waved his muzzle towards the safe. Bond sighed and opened it once again. Carson counted the money. Then he spoke.

"If I ever come back this way don't start with me, Bond. I'm feelin' grateful to you just now because you put me in the way of this fifty-seven thousand. So we'll just let this here matter of my treatment by the general drop. But I'll be mighty touchy where you're concerned. An' I aim to be around in Texas a long time. Better lock up yore safe. The money in there looks mighty temptin'."

"Lucky you're honest," growled Bond.

"*Vaya con Dios*," said Carson. He blew out the light on the table and closed the door. He thought of Bond sitting there in the darkness thinking. He grinned. The moon had set. Somewhere off in the dark town a dog was barking, over and over. He thought of Luisa asleep with her hand on the butt of his Colt. He smiled. She could keep it, he had two more.

Chapter Seventeen

"Which way you gonna go?" asked Bearclaw.

"Up the Blanco."

"Why the Blanco? Why not—"

"There's good fresh water there," Carson said. "We're goin' up the Blanco."

"Yeah," said Archie, "but if there's good water there, there'll be Comanches there too."

"And—?" asked Carson, coldly.

"Jeez, maybe there'll be 'paches there too. I hear them Comanches come down thataway every moon to steal horses."

"You want to leave?" said Carson. He buckled on his right spur and stood up. "Take your horse and ride."

"Four hundred miles alone through Indian country? That ain't practical."

"Then shut up an' do what I say. Bearclaw, you and Sebastiano will start off as pointers. Archie, you an' Ricardo will take the drags—"

"The drags?"

"Each mornin' we'll rotate. We'll all take our turns swallowin' dust. I'll start off with the swing. Don't let 'em bunch up. Keep 'em 'bout fifty-sixty feet across, no longer than half a mile. It looks hard, but after a couple days the critters'll get used to it then it'll get easier all around. Don't let 'em trot. They'll try to do that to fill up spaces—and that trottin'll just burn off good beef. Well, boys, go out an' learn the cow business."

For once Archie had nothing to say. He rode out part of the way with Bearclaw. "You hear what he said 'bout them Comanches? They'll eat us raw, raw without salt!" There was a drumming of hooves behind them. They turned. It was Carson.

"I don't want any fires after dusk. We'll stop and eat

while there's still plenty of light. Use buff'lo chips for fires
—no smoke. Your carbines loaded?"

"What good would they be if they ain't loaded?" asked
Archie contemptuously. Carson said patiently, "Check."

"I don't have to check," Archie said, sullen.

Carson leaned over and pulled out Archie's carbine from
its scabbard. He worked the lever. It was empty. He handed
it back silently. Bearclaw guffawed. "Archie the Great forgot!" he chortled. Archie silently and viciously shoved cartridges into his carbine, staring with hatred at the receding
Carson.

"I know what you'd like to do," Bearclaw observed. "But
that Valdes gang likes Carson, and they ain't dumb. You
better play it cool till we get back and they get shipped
home. King Fisher'll have his cattle an' his money all in
one place an' what happens then won't concern him. An'
you can count on me, cousin. We're blood kin, you 'n me.
I just don't want to leave my scalp dryin' in some Comanche lodge. So you better make double sure you got that
thing loaded—"

"Agh, shut up, you fat tub of guts!" Bearclaw grinned and
pulled up his bandanna to keep the thickening dust out of his
nose and mouth.

Luisa preferred to ride rather than sit in the wagon. She
would ride silently beside old Valdes. Then she would drop
back and ride beside Carson. She avoided talking to him.
She would look at him quietly. Carson had the feeling she
was waiting for the proper moment to tell him something.
He waited for her to bring it up. He gave no sign of impatience. Once he asked her if she would like to go to
Santa Fe—there were many old Spanish families—certainly
there would be someone there who knew the de Parrals? She
nodded but refused his offer to put her on the stage for Santa
Fe. She rode silently and expertly.

What did she want? Once she said, with passion so sudden
that he almost spilled his coffee, that she would like to have
every peon on her hacienda killed and new ones brought
in. He leaned back against the wagon wheel and smoked a
cigarette, staring at her. She added that then she would go
back and rule the ancient hacienda. Almost panting with her
excitement she stood up and walked till she stood almost
touching him.

"You come back with me," she said, gripping his arm and

digging her nails into his muscle. "We raise an army. We kill the general and Pablo. It will be easy. No, maybe not easy. But we do it—" she paused and took a deep breath. "Then you marry me. And you will own the hacienda. Eh?"

Carson started to laugh but checked himself. She was deadly serious and would not forgive laughter.

"Six hundred peons!" she said. She would not kill them, she had changed her mind. But they needed a strong hand. She released his arm but held his hand with both of hers. Carson was touched by the gesture, so child-like, but so serious and so deadly. He did not want to hurt her feelings, she had suffered enough; she had tried to help him when he was helpless, when there was nothing to gain by it but a blow across her face with a quirt.

She was looking up into his face, trying to see what his decision would be. There would be a moon soon; it was still under the ridge that rose to the east, covered with scrub juniper. She reached up and took off his sombrero to see his face. He laughed, touched by the earnest childishness of the gesture. She slapped his face.

He grabbed her wrist, furious.

"You don't believe me, *Tejano?*"

Once more he was in a good humor—her calling him that had done it. He released her. She rubbed her wrist. He was sorry; he had not realized how angry he had been. He tried to make amends.

"Sure, sure, I believe you."

"You want to think? I go away, I sleep. Tomorrow you answer, yes?"

"All right," Carson said.

All the next day Carson thought over her offer. He began to think about it right after breakfast. He thought about it at first because he had promised. But the more he thought about it the less idiotic it seemed to him. The essence of it seemed to be that if he killed the general and Pablo she would then marry him. He did not need an army for that. He could do it himself. He would have to be very, very careful how he did it, but it was possible. Getting away afterwards would take some skillful planning and some very good horses. It would all take money and time. He had the money—fifty-seven thousand dollars of it. And it was the general who had made the acquisition of the money possible.

"What you laughin' at?" said Archie.

He had not realized he was laughing aloud.

"You goin' crazy, Carson," said Archie.

He whirled his horse and pelted down a hill to rescue a cow that had gotten herself stuck in a bog. Carson followed. The two of them dropped their riatas over her horns and pulled her out. When she got on her feet she tried to hook Carson's horse. When he had finished driving her back to the herd Archie said, "Looky here, remember, you bust your ass tryin' to help that pore cow an' she tried to kill you. That's all the gratitude you kin expect from any female." He grinned and trotted off.

Well, Carson thought, so the little son-of-a-bitch was listening in last night. But maybe he had a point there. He would think his way around that.

If the hacienda had good grass and water—and he could use some of that fifty-seven thousand to buy good bulls and try to develop a heat-resistant strain—and if he were the legal owner—and if no one in her family tried to stop him —he almost shouted with excitement. He could become the wealthiest rancher in Sonora! He would come up to San Antonio once a year and buy silver-trimmed saddles and Arab stock.

He saw two small branches, broken, hanging about a foot from the end. They had been broken by someone on horseback. His eyes went to the ground. There were two crossed sticks directly below them. One stick lay along the trail but the other pointed up a side canyon. His face hardened. He pulled his Winchester from the scabbard and very carefully rode up the canyon. It was a small box canyon. Nothing was there.

Every night, as soon as the north star became visible, Carson pointed the wagon tongue at it; if the next morning would be raining or cloudy the tongue would be useful as a compass. In this way he would be able to start the herd off in the right direction. The night was chilly. Carson had taken the first watch. When it was almost over he saw a campfire burning brightly in the hollow they had camped in for the night. He rode hard for the camp and kicked it out without saying a word.

"Who made it?" he asked.

Archie looked at him. "Don't blame them Valdes boys," he said. "I did it. They was gonna object but I started twirlin' the cylinder on my Colt so they shut up. I was gettin' cold, that's why I lit it."

"Well, I'll tell you what you done," said Carson. "You just published a big extra edition for every goddam Comanche for miles around to read. Speakin' for me, I don't give a goddam if they spread you on an ant-hill and work you over with their lances, but I need every man to get this herd to your uncle. You do somethin' like this once more and I am gonna tie you up and haul you back like a sack of potatoes. The Valdes boys are with me, so it's four against two. I'm gettin' sick of spankin' you a little at a time. Next time you're gonna get it good." He turned and walked away.

A little after sunrise a war party went south several hundred yards away. They had ten loose horses. They halted and sang a war song and waved something on a pole.

"What's that?" asked Bearclaw.

"They want us to think it's a scalp."

Bearclaw turned towards Archie. "You damn runt!" he shouted. " 'I'm cold, I'm cold,' " he whimpered, in a falsetto. He turned to Carson again.

"I will consider it a scalp," Carson said dryly. Archie showed not the slightest sign of fear. He had run to the wagon, pulled out his Springfield, and was sighting it. Carson reached him just in time to knock the barrel upwards. The bullet screeched harmlessly upwards.

Carson grabbed the barrel with his right hand. With his left he slapped Archie. Sebastiano grabbed Archie's right hand as it went for his Colt. The war song had stopped. The lance with the scalp was lowered. For a second the horses stood out against the sky; then they suddenly disappeared. They had vanished, except for the tip of a lance that flashed in the sun. Then that disappeared.

"If we're very lucky," said Carson, "they'll forget about us. They had a good scrap and were satisfied enough to boast a bit. Then they were gonna ride past. Now maybe they'll reconsider." He turned to Sebastiano. "Tie him up," he said in Spanish. "*Con mucho gusto*," said Sebastiano, who pulled a piece of rawhide from his saddlebag.

After an hour he ordered Archie released. Archie ate a swift sullen breakfast and rode off. By mid-morning his active resentment had simmered down to a steady banked fire that he would keep under control until the situation would arrive where he could blow on it with all the force of his hatred. Until then he would keep out of trouble, especially where the odds were so obviously against him.

He rode his horse down a slope covered with small loose stones. At the bottom the horse gathered his legs for the scramble up the other side. At the top five Comanche warriors were sitting their horses.

No one moved. Archie froze.

"Good horse," one said, staring at Archie's horse. "A very good horse. You take mine. Me take yours." Archie said nothing.

"No care swap horses?"

Archie shook his head. He was afraid to trust his voice.

"Gimme cartuches." The bad Spanish meant nothing to Archie but the gesture was clear: the Comanche had pointed to his cartridge belt.

Archie shook his head again.

The Comanche looked at him impassively.

"You give beef?"

One of the Comanches began to circle around to Archie's rear. The wind sprang up and stirred the feathers on their shields. Archie felt the sweat breaking out on his face in spite of the cool wind. He could feel it sliding down his back between his shoulder blades.

The dry thock! of a carbine lever being worked came from behind a boulder. The Comanches spun around. A muzzle pointed at them. Sebastiano's voice said, "*Anda, anda!*"

The Comanches slowly turned and slowly rode away.

Carson rode down a draw looking for three cattle. He found them and started forcing them back to the trail. But he caught a glimpse of something black sliding between the rocks of a spur. At first he thought it was a crow that had sailed between the rocks. He rode on. Around the bend the narrow valley opened up into a pleasant park. A quarter of a mile ahead he saw the same five warriors who had had the run-in with Sebastiano. They were still irritated. They had taken plenty of horses on their raid and a few scalps, and were not in the mood to risk being shot in an effort to take anything from well-armed and determined men, but that was their mood of the morning. Now they were a little touchy.

Carson halted and grasped his horse's nose lest it whinny to the Indian ponies.

But one warrior turned and saw him. The five horses stopped. They turned and began trotting towards him. He waved them around. They paid no attention. His horse was exhausted. Theirs were fresh. He chose to fight on high ground rather than be bottled up, and he rode to high ground, turned, and dropped a couple of bullets ahead of their horses. But they came on.

As a final warning he knocked up dust under the lead horse's nose and then slipped in three cartridges for business purposes. He took off his sombrero and filled it full of cartridges.

One of the Comanches fired. The bullet came up where he was with a long heart-rending squeal and went spat! against the wall a few feet from his head, while the great cliff back of him bellowed. Then they went to cover. One of them grabbed the reins of all the horses and pulled them down into a gully.

"Aaaagh!" one of the warriors shouted. "*Perro Tejano!* Coward! Shoot, shoot!"

Carson grinned and took a pull at his canteen. Sooner or later they would get bored with this and either charge or go home. He settled down for a wait.

Luisa was riding beside Ricardo, who was driving the wagon that day. She was sweating and dusty. A little valley opened up to the right. Deep inside, a mile away, she saw trees and a little waterfall. She reined up, and headed that way.

"*Adonde vaya usted, Señorita?*"

She told Ricardo she wanted to take a bath.

"Señor Carson would not like it."

She did not consider this worth an answer and showed it by riding away. She found a rocky pool and stripped and swam while her horse grazed. Then she dressed and began to braid her hair, while she looked for her coral necklace. She was sure it had fallen into a crevice between two rocks, and while she twisted her damp hair she peered downwards, looking for it.

An old squaw stepped forth confidently from the bushes, followed by a girl. They wore buckskin skirts and leggings. The girl, who was twelve, wore a bracelet and necklace made of large chunks of turquoise.

The old squaw came up to Luisa and began to complain

about her intrusion. She waved her hand low over the ground
and then looked angrily at the horse. Luisa guessed at her
meaning: the horse was eating up all the grass. The girl
circled around Luisa, staring at her clothes. She found the
coral necklace, and with a pleased grin put it on over her
own blue one. Then she squatted at the pool and looked at
her reflection with delight. The old woman kept complaining
in a monotone that Luisa soon found irritating. Luisa stood
up and went on with her braiding. Neither of the women had
washed for some time and the smell was strong.

The old squaw's voice became quite shrill. Luisa waved
her away and made sign that the girl could keep her necklace, but this did not put the squaw in a good humor.

Luisa felt her belt lighten. She turned around. The girl had
stepped behind her and was trying to steal her Colt. The girl
let it drop back into the holster and grinned.

The squaw began to complain once more. Luisa faced her.
Every time she felt her belt lighten she looked around at the
girl, who again let it drop back into the holster.

She began again. Luisa turned and made a face. The girl
recoiled, startled, and then began to laugh. When Luisa had
turned her back the girl made her boldest attempt at the gun.
Luisa had had enough. She made a swift catch without looking and caught the little squaw's wrist. The girl gave a supple
twist and broke her bracelet, which came off in Luisa's hand.
Some of the beads rolled between the rocks and some fell
into the pool and sank to the bottom. The squaw was furious
and aimed a slap at Luisa's face, but the blow fell on her
shoulder.

Luisa stepped back and drew her Colt and pretended to
shoot.

The old squaw immediately plunged into the bushes, followed by the weeping girl. Luisa called after her, telling her
to come back and take her beads.

But there was no answer. The branches stopped rustling
and there was no sound but the wind blowing across the tops
of the trees. She moved closer, calling. She parted the bushes.
Three feet in front of her two warriors stood. They grinned
and began moving towards her. She turned and ran for her
horse.

"Vamoose, vamoose, no hurt!" one called out.

The horse was gone. His hoof prints in the dust were
half-blotted out by moccasin prints. She ran as fast as she

could through the canyon. The two men followed at an easy lope.

As she ran she thought that perhaps they were sure she had no bullets in her Colt. She stopped, lifted it, and fired in the air. She was right. They halted, surprised. Neither was armed, except that the closer one had a knife at his waist. He put his hand on the hilt, but as she cocked the Colt again he froze. She began walking, holding the Colt, and turning every few steps to look at them. They didn't move. One folded his arms. Behind him the girl appeared with a tear-stained face and shook her fist at Luisa.

Luisa's shot sounded against the cliff where Carson lay. The Comanches halted and conferred quickly. Their women were in that direction. Two of them fired quickly at him and turned to leave. One rose high in his stirrups and turning his rear towards Carson, slapped it in derision. Carson restrained himself with difficulty from trying a snap shot at it.

"All we lost today is a horse and a necklace," Carson said. "Any other damage?"

"Obvious they don't want a fight." He turned to Luisa. "Good thing you fired in the air, or they'd hang around and lift one scalp to get even."

"What're they after?" asked Bearclaw.

"Maybe stragglers. But we're gonna find out fast." He nodded to the ridge ahead. Far ahead, on its crest, a warrior was galloping his horse in tight little circles. "He wants to make peace talk. Archie, get out the blunderbuss. We might have to play our old game again."

He rode out.

The Comanche sat his horse and waited. He wore a full war bonnet, but Carson was glad to see that he did not have on the formal war paint across his face. He held a lance. Nine scalps fluttered from it. When Carson halted a few feet away he could see that three were fresh. Across his bare chest he wore a carbine cartridge belt. Carson noticed that it held only six cartridges. That, then, was the reason why the Comanches had been so restrained.

The warrior began talking sign.

There was no buffalo. They were hungry. They would like to buy cartridges. Then they would go to the higher ranges and shoot deer. Winter was coming, they had to jerk deer and

make pemmican. He would pay a dollar apiece for cartridges. Behind him two more men appeared. Then the two
women; Carson realized that the girl was sitting on Luisa's
horse. He noticed that they all seemed thin. He shook his
head.

"Me got money," said the chief. He beckoned the old squaw
up. He pointed at her buckskin pouch which she wore slung
over her shoulder. She opened it and the chief reached in and
pulled out a handful of crumpled greenbacks. Carson saw
they were real and not the souvenir coupons so often handed
to Indians.

There was blood on quite a few of them, and a few bullet
holes with scorched edges. Carson shook his head. He had
not the slightest desire to sell someone some cartridges when
they would be coming back at him a few hours later.

He offered them two cattle as a gift. No cartridges. Perhaps they would be amused to know that all his men were
expert shots. At this distance, for instance, any one of them
could put a hole through a silver dollar.

The chief grinned. He made the negative sign. He estimated
the distance from the wagon and the group around it, and
then he rotated his right forefinger around his right ear.

"Here we go again," said Carson under his breath. He
held up a silver dollar. This time he held on firmly and did
not lose his grip on it when the bullet tugged at it.

The chief's face lost its amused look. He stared with respect towards the tiny puff of smoke. Carson tossed the hol-
lowed dollar to the girl, who caught it and began to string it
on the coral necklace.

Carson made sign. He wanted the necklace and the horse.
If not, no beef. The chief did not change expression. He was
counting the number that faced him. He might pick them off
one by one, Carson knew he was thinking, but then his warriors had very little ammunition, and the whites were excellent shots. The risks were too great.

The chief turned and spoke in the harsh Comanche tongue.
The girl refused to give up her horse or to yield the necklace. The chief was not having any back talk. He ripped off
her necklace and pushed her violently out of her saddle.

In tears the girl screamed at him while the other Comanches laughed. The chief gave the necklace and the reins of the
horse to Carson. He tossed the silver dollar to the girl. She
stopped sobbing long enough to fling it back at him and then

she hurled herself at him and began striking his leg with her fist. He pushed her away; she came back again at the end of his arm and bit his hand. He rode off, rubbing his hand while the Comanches chuckled.

When he had arrived at the wagon he told Sebastiano to cut out two good beeves and let the Comanches have them. As the men trotted off he gave the necklace to Luisa. She played with the coral chunks, not looking at him.

"Carson," she said.

He turned.

"I like what you do. You make a very good *hacendero*. You come back to Isleta, we—"

"No."

"Three hundred fifty years ago, Carson," she said, "you make a very good conquistador." She turned her back to him and held out the necklace. "You fix?"

He put it on. She leaned back against him and looked over her shoulder at him. He looked down at her and his heart began to beat quickly. She felt it and smiling, let her head fall back, and mouth half-opened, she waited.

She moaned with the pain of the fierce kiss, pulled her mouth away, shook her head, excited, and as his mouth came down again, she murmured, "Isleta?"

"No," he murmured, and turned her around to face him.

"Cobarde!" she said, and shoved him violently. He staggered back a step and his spur caught in a saddle that had been flung on the ground. He fell backwards as a shadow fell across him.

"Told you any cow you pull out of a bog would hook you in the guts first chance she got," said Archie. "You owe me five bucks."

"For what?" asked Carson, furious. He stood up.

"You promised me five if I clipped that silver dollar dead center at the island."

Carson gave him the money.

Chapter Eighteen

"Good stock," said King Fisher, approvingly. They rode through the rest of the herd and up the grassy slope. They halted at a live oak. It was hot and there was no wind. King Fisher dismounted and squatted in the shade. Carson followed him; his back was still paining him and his face showed it. The skin across the bridge of his nose had still not healed. King Fisher eyed his slow movements shrewdly but said nothing.

"Look at them buggers eat," he said. "By God, they got that pasture clipped like a lawn. Move 'em north tomorrow. They didn't lose too much coming up north. You're a good cowman, Carson."

"Thanks."

"Another two hundred pounds on 'em and we'll take 'em up to Dodge. Heard you had a rough time in Mexico." Carson nodded.

In exactly the same mildly sympathetic tone King Fisher added, "And they say you're a cow thief."

"They say the same thing about you, Mr. Fisher."

King Fisher grinned. "You ain't afraid of me at all."

"No."

"Heard you paid off your mortgage in full yestiddy."

"You heard right."

"Some people say you paid it off with my money, Carson."

"It all depends on how you look at it."

"I look at it like maybe they're right," said King Fisher lazily, and he got up and mounted. "So don't you figger you owe me a polite thank you?"

Carson rode silently beside him. After a moment he replied, "No."

"How come?" asked King Fisher, amused. "If it wasn't

116

for me you'd still be grubbin' around with a lousy herd of
mebbe seventy, eighty scrubs, all built like jackrabbits,
crawlin' with screwworm, bawlin' for water, each worth
mebbe four bucks. How'd you be able to tie 'em up with
that forty-dollar market at Dodge or Abilene? How'd you
take 'em across that dry country full of 'paches if you was
gonna try to sell 'em to the miners up in the Mogollones?
You couldn't afford to hire no one to trail 'em to Arizona
or up north." He lit a cigar. "No one at all. At all."

He looked at Carson, waiting.

Carson said, "I worked for you two days in Mexico. I
figger I get all that I can get once you get the twenty
head you bargained for."

King Fisher smiled. "You think you're a hard man. Remember this: I don't travel like a colt no more, but if you
think you'll hold the handles for me, there ain't no chance
for that. I'll be the one that will let you down easy with my
hat off."

"I'll remember that, Mr. King Fisher."

King Fisher shrugged, looking at the end of his cigar. He
took a deep breath, and taking his sombrero off, swept it
around the horizon. The sweep took in the big corrals, the
windmills, the cattle sprinkled like specks of cinnamon over
the richly grassed hills and gentle valleys. "Big an' pretty!
Big an' pretty!" he said. "But hot damn, wouldn't it be fun
to tear her down an' start all over again?"

"Put on your hat, Mr. King Fisher," Carson said dryly.
"You'll get sunstroke."

"If I ain't got it already, eh? I bet you don't understand
what the hell I'm talkin' about." He put on his sombrero,
and went on, with a chuckle. "You're makin' me a lot of
trouble, boy. This de Parral girl who's fixin' to throw her
shoes under your bed—" Carson stiffened. "Lemme finish,
boy. I don't like a woman hangin' around here unless she's
married. She's got everyone bellerin' an' pawin' up dust. I
seen Archie hangin' round her room as nervous as a
cockroach on a hot skillet. She ain't married, you ain't
staked out a claim on her—everyone figgers he's a got a
right to service the lady. No offense meant. I don't want
shootin' startin' over her."

"I'll take her over to my place tomorrow. Didn't want
to till I got it fixed up a bit."

"Hope she ain't crazy. Don' look at me thataway. She sits there all day an' won't say a word."

"She ain't crazy."

"She acks like some woman I saw after the Indians got finished with her."

"I tell you she ain't crazy."

"I knocked at her door this mornin'. No answer. Wanted to find out if she slept comfortable and would like another blanket. No answer. Knocked again. Pushed the door open. She sat in the rockin' chair with that Colt you gave her in her lap. She jus' pointed that cannon at me an' at the door. Moved it less than an inch. I closed that door as soft as anyone could wish. I don't argue with someone with that look in their face. I don't want that woman runnin' around here with that .45. Sooner or later cousin Archie is gonna go in for some fancy huggin' an' if she don't wanna be hugged cousin Archie is gonna be very dead. If she was mine I'd slap that gun out of her hand and then paddle her bottom. But then I'd have trouble with you. Jus' tellin' you, boy, so's you can handle it peaceful."

"She'll be gone tomorrow."

"Also watch yourself goin' to town. My family is goin' around pawin' up the ground somethin' fierce at the idea of you makin' yourself a heap of money out of this last deal of mine. They figger it's Fisher money."

"You figger it's Fisher money?"

"We been through that, boy. Let's say you earned it. Wish you hadn't been so hard on Bond. With them prices you put on the carbines he'll come squallin' to me. If I wanna do more business with him I'll jus' have to pay him back everythin' above a fair market price." He grinned. "But I don't mind. It's time someone rubbed his nose in the ground a bit. This de Parral woman, you thinkin' of marryin' her?"

"No."

"You like her more than you'll admit. Maybe more than you'll admit to yourself. I can tell by the way you look at her. You know much about women?"

Carson shook his head.

"She looks like the kind made for this country. My wife wasn't. We weren't married jus' two months an' over in Kenyon they caught two horse thieves. My wife said 'I understand they hanged them to a telegraph pole.' I couldn't think of anythin' to say, I was involved in it—she looked so mad I decided to keep quiet. All I came out with was, 'Well, I don't think it hurt the telegraph pole none.' She said, 'I used to think I knew you in Louisiana but you have been out so long among the Yankees and Ruffians till I don't know whether I know you or not. I want you to take me back to Louisiana, I won't live in such a country.' It was hard holdin' her, but when the baby came she was all right."

They were riding by the old cemetery. Carson noticed that King Fisher averted his face. Carson was sure that King Fisher did not want to open old wounds by seeing the gravestones of his wife and son.

When they had ridden past he went on. "That de Parral woman looks strong. She can handle a gun. My wife wouldn't go near one. And she looks like good stock. Mebbe part Indian. I seen breeds with blue eyes up in the Dakotas. You don't mind a bunch of quarter-breeds runnin' around? With her for a dam the stock ought to improve." King Fisher grinned at Carson's growing irritation.

"You ain't goin' after the general?" King Fisher said, looking at Carson's hard-set profile.

"No."

"You ain't takin' up her dare."

"I ain't crazy."

"Maybe not so crazy. You spread the right flavor honey an' he'll come buzzin' around. When he gets his feet all sticky—" King Fisher slapped his palm hard against his thigh—"Squush!" His horse skittered sidewards a bit at the sudden sound, but King Fisher brought her back easily.

"And then?"

"Wait a minute. You gotta get him out of Mexico. You ain't gonna make the Rio Grande at a run three times in a row, that's pushin' your luck. You gotta get him alone. That'll be hard, he likely won't go alone anywhere, he'll travel with a couple of men for a bodyguard. An' with that Pablito, there's a hard case. Archie says he lost an eye an' broke some teeth account of you."

"He fired my carbine when the barrel was full of dried mud. Tried to warn him not to."

"Don' matter. It's your carbine, right? An' how does he know you were gonna warn 'im? Jus' your word. So he's gonna lay for you. Jeez, Carson, you got *everyone* layin' for you, 'cept me, I guess. An' that don't mean much. I always disagreed with everyone else. Well, back to the general. You gotta think up some way to get 'im alone."

They halted and dismounted. Sebastiano came up and took their horses. King Fisher watched him take them to the corral and get their feed ready. "Good man, that Valdes," he said, lazily. "You trust 'im?"

"Why shouldn't I?" asked Carson, surprised.

"Can't tell when he'll turn on you, that's why," King Fisher said. "Ain't that your experience with Mexicans?"

Carson stared at King Fisher's face, trying to pry a meaning out of the calmly smiling surface.

"This Valdes—he ain't a sort of friend of the general?"

"Not likely."

"He ain't here an' sort of reportin' back on your next move, is he?"

"Not unless he's a mighty good actor."

"Better be sure you keep your thinkin' a secret from him when you work out your spider web. You'll need a couple good men you can trust. A hundred dollars apiece is gonna look good to some poor Mexicans. Even if they like the general, a hundred dollars in gold looks mighty good. 'An' if all works out all right you'll wind up the biggest *hacendero* in Sonora. With your knowhow in the cattle business, an' your speakin' Mex pretty good, you could be a big man down there. All you need is a good idea an' some luck."

King Fisher threw his cigar stub away.

"Don't appeal to you, eh?"

"It still don't appeal."

"All right. No more. Get the men an' move the general's cows to the north pasture. We'll start brandin' tomorrow."

King Fisher watched Carson ride away. He lit another cigar very slowly, as he always did when he was thinking very hard. He thought his plan for dealing with the general an excellent one. He could punch no holes in it anywhere. As a matter of fact, it appealed to him so much he was going to do it himself.

Chapter Nineteen

Late next afternoon King Fisher lay in his hammock, relaxing after a day's hard riding. He had already killed one-third of a bottle of bourbon while Carson was still sipping his second drink.

"I admire a man's built hisself up as fast as you, Carson," King Fisher said, thickly. "Takes brains." He sat up, straddled the hammock, and shifted to a nearby chair. He poured himself another glassful.

"An' takes a sharp eye. Pour yourself another drink, boy!"

Carson filled his glass and drank it slowly.

"An' takes somethin' else. Archie, commere!"

"Whaddya want?"

"Don't mumble when you talk to me, boy. Get here fast."

Archie slouched up and leaned against one of the oak beams. He picked away at a dirty fingernail.

"Sit down, boy."

Archie sat.

"Now stand up."

Archie stood, baffled and irritated.

"Sit down." Archie glowered and sat.

King Fisher turned to Carson.

"Stand up." Carson didn't move.

"You heard me, boy. Stand up!"

Carson sipped his bourbon.

"Why aincha standin' when I say so?"

"You better stop drinkin' if you wanna fight, King Fisher."

Archie swallowed with excitement and backed out of the way.

King Fisher stood. He wavered, but steadied himself by laying a hand against the pillar.

"I'm standin'," he said slowly. "You got any objection to standin' now?"

Carson shrugged, put his glass down carefully, and stood up. King Fisher moved his heavy shoulders under his shirt as if he were limbering up. His right hand flashed to his inlaid butt.

Carson's hand was on his butt a fraction of a second before.

"An it takes one more thing," added King Fisher. "Takes guts." He took his hand off his butt and sagged back into the hammock. Archie's face hardened with disappointment.

"Get us some more whisky, boy," King Fisher said, his forefinger idly tracing the silver card patterns on the butt. "We're gonna have us a tea-party."

"You're lookin' to git yourself kilt," said Dave next morning. "You're hung over bad, aincha?"

King Fisher growled.

"That Carson, he don't look like much, King Fisher," Dave went on, disregarding King Fisher's obvious headache. "He drinks but he don't lose control. But you do. An' once, that's all it takes, just once, you're gonna push 'im too far and he's gonna get his in first. Mark my words."

"I ain't markin' your words. Get me some coffee."

"You kept gettin' more and more drunk. You disremember?"

"I don't remember nothin', teacher."

"You better watch yourself. Your tadpole ass has got an urge to outtalk your crocodile mouth. I'll tell you what happened. Every half-hour you'd race 'im to see whose hand reached whose gun butt first. He allus won. Then the both of you'd have a drink an' try again. He was drinkin' as much as you was, too. He wasn't spillin' any either under the table like a dance-hall girl. You mought like him an' all, but some day he'll blow a hole in you big enough for a blind man to piss through. You better watch yourself."

"If I watched myself," said King Fisher, holding his head with his eyes closed, "I'd be a broken-down cowpuncher shovelin' horseshit in a livery stable somewhere. I ain't never watched myself, an' that's why you got a job with me, and that's why Archie's got a job with me, and that's why you bunch of lousy bummers is gonna inherit the biggest damn corrals around here, an' that's why I ship more cattle to

Dodge than anyone else in this part of Texas. An' that's why I like this Carson feller. He don't watch hisself neither. He puts all his chips down an' he rides it all the way until the wheel stops rollin' and now get the hell outahere. My head's killin' me."

"I'm tellin' you, you better watch out, that Carson feller ain't—"

"It's never no mind for me. Lemme tell you somethin'. I like a man who fights with everythin' he's got. Las' night I ran Archie ragged makin' him sit down and stand up. He took it. An' he ain't got nothin' to lose. An' he took it! You think I get any satisfaction out of makin' that pup do tricks? I got me a man now who does the hard things I tell 'im without cryin' on my shoulder. He's a hard man an' he's smart. I'm tellin' you it's gettin' to be a pleasure for me tryin' to outsmart him. I gotta be light on my feet for that. An' the exercise is good for this here ol' bull."

He drank some coffee. "I remember my Bible. Someone in it said, 'no athlete without sweat is crowned!' That's me, Dave."

"I don't know what you're talkin' about," Dave said, impatiently. "All I say is, better gun 'im down 'fore he gits too big for his britches. He's beginnin' to act the turkey rooster. He's after that de Parral *mujer,* an' you, you damn fool, you think you got yourself a hen, spreadin' that tail an' gobblin' to yourself! It's time someone pulled out a couple of his tail feathers. Just on gen'ral principles. Crissake, how's it gonna look if you an' him tangle over some Mex chippy? I got a mind to pull out a handful myself."

"You just do that little thing," said King Fisher softly, plunging his head into a bucket of water. He pulled his great dripping head out, and looking like a massive sea god, fumbled blindly for a towel. Dave threw him one, angrily. King Fisher chuckled and went on, "Yep, you try it. You won't live long enough to eject your used cartridge."

Chapter Twenty

Valdes had brought a guitar with him. In the evenings he played. An old man singing love songs! Carson was amused at the thought. But nevertheless, he would lean against the rough trunk of one of the old cottonwoods and listen. There was something about Mexican songs sung to a guitar in the cool dark after a burning day choking on dust that moved and stirred even him, in a way that songs sung in English could not. Valdes did not play well; his voice was too reedy, but the songs had passion, and his longing for his wife found an outlet in them.

The song ended. The guitar was silent a moment. Then it began again, very sure, much better played. A woman began singing, in a warm, husky contralto:

> Que lejos de mi tierra
> de mi alma el dueño!
> Que lejos los labios
> que beso en mi sueño!

> How far away is my love,
> How far away the lips I kiss
> in my dreams!

Carson's match broke. Before he could strike another a flame was burning several inches in front of him.

"Sings pretty good, don't she?"

Carson lit his cigarette and watched King Fisher light his cigar. Carson nodded. He was aware of a savage resentment—he realized, half-amused, half-seriously, that he didn't want to share her singing.

She went on:

> Pienso que escucho al son
> de su caballo!

Me despierto—pero es nadie—
y me callo.

I think I hear his horse—
I wake up—but it is no one,
And I am silent.

"Man who lassoes that," observed King Fisher, "is gonna have one hell of a time holdin' her down, even if he slaps his brand on 'er. That one's *muy mujer*. G'night."

"Goodnight," Carson said. He had decided he would like very much to put his brand on her.

Archie and Bearclaw were leaning against the other side of the corral, staring at her. Archie had a pack of cards stuck in his hip pocket. His left hand still held some poker chips. She leaned her head back, took a deep breath, and sang again. Her breasts thrust against the thin cotton dress, and even in the moonlight, under the dark cloud of her hair, with the yellow light from the lantern ringing her, Carson could see her throat pulse and swell as she sang. He turned aside and began to walk slowly away. He wanted to think things out very clearly. He was going to make some very delicate moves very soon, and the chips he was betting with would be his life and hers.

"What's she singin' about?" asked Archie. He was a little drunk.

"Some guy left 'er an' she wants to die," said Bearclaw.

"Don't make sense," said Archie. He shoved the pack of cards deeper into his hip pocket. "Tell you what'll make sense." He stared hungrily at her breasts.

Bearclaw caught the glance. "Yeah, me too," he said, "but King Fisher, I seen him lookin' her over too. You wanna tangle with a buzz saw that's related to a rattlesnake?"

"What you talkin' about? She wants it, only no one's smart enough to see it."

"An' you're smart enough?"

"Yeah. Watch me."

He left abruptly and came back with two other cowpunchers he had been gambling with. He had buckled on his gun belt and was weaving slightly.

"Keep quiet," he said. "I'll handle her right. Nobody say nothin'. She won't recognize us if we all keep our mouths shut."

They watched her hand the guitar over to Valdes. When she had reached the end of the corral fence Archie stepped behind her. She heard his step and whirled around, lifting her arms. Bearclaw grabbed her arms from behind as Archie crammed his bandanna into her mouth and tied it in place with another one handed to him by one of the other men. With a short piece of rope Bearclaw tied her arms behind her back. She struggled and choked on the filthy bandanna, and kicked out violently. By chance she caught Bearclaw in the solar plexus. His explosive grunt of agony carried to Carson.

Carson listened. Dismissing it as a muffled snort from one of the horses in the corral, he resumed his walking.

One of the men stumbled and dropped her leg. She kicked hard as he straightened up and the point of her shoe caught him under the chin. His muffled yelp of surprise came clearly to Carson this time.

He turned and began walking warily towards the sound.

Archie hissed, "Keep walkin' with 'er!" They struggled on. Archie slipped behind a cottonwood. As Carson came by Archie whipped the barrel of his Colt downward. Carson caught the rustle of his clothes and had just enough time to pull his head to one side. The barrel crashed downwards onto his shoulder, paralyzing his right arm. He hooked his left into Archie's ribs and then wrapped his hand around Archie's gun hand. He was about to twist the gun out of his grip when a heavy fist struck the back of his neck. Now, almost completely paralyzed, he fell forward onto his face. He heard footsteps running up. Boots began kicking him in his back, in his face, in his stomach. He had not enough strength to cover himself with his arms. A boot crashed into his mouth. No one spoke. His mouth filled with a warm salty fluid. Blood. He heard the men panting and grunting as they kicked. He tried to mark them in some way but he had not the strength.

They stopped.

"He ain't movin'," he heard someone whisper.

"Think the son-of-a-bitch is dead?"

Someone held his head up and peered into it. "Looks like it," a voice said, with satisfaction. His head was brutally dropped with a thud into the dust.

"We better get outta here," a voice said.

"What about the girl?"

"After the funeral."

They laughed and Carson heard footsteps moving away. He turned his head for a good look at them but it was too dark. He pressed his face into the dust and spat out blood, waiting for his muscles to do what he willed them to. It would take a few minutes yet, he knew. He heard footsteps coming toward him. He closed his eyes and braced himself for a kick.

Luisa's voice said warily, *"Quien está?"*

"Yo," Carson managed to say.

"Did they hurt you?"

"They did pretty good."

"Can you untie me?"

"You better get down."

She sat with her back to him. He managed to untie her but he needed his teeth to help. When she was free she pulled him from under the tree into the moonlight. He heard her sharp intake of breath.

"I don't look so good, eh?"

With her help he was able to get to her room. She lit her lantern and washed his face. It was badly swollen and getting worse. There were several cuts due to the sharp-toed boots. He ached all over and he knew he would ache worse in the morning. He fell asleep. When he woke up the lantern had been put out, and the morning light was beginning to streak the heavy oak planks out of which the shutters were made. He turned and looked at her.

She was asleep, on her back, one arm flung over her head in an unconscious imitation of a Spanish dancer; the other arm was bent at the right elbow with the palm resting on her flat stomach. She had put on a blue cotton nightgown that buttoned primly up to her throat. He could see where her nipples strained against the thin cotton. His eyes moved down her flat stomach, over where her hips flared against the taut cotton, and down the long thighs and calves to her slender brown ankles. When his eyes travelled back to the tightly buttoned top of her gown he suddenly became aware of her amused stare.

He flushed.

She placed one palm on top of the other, like a slender brown goddess. Her breathing quickened. He felt his rough, unshaven, cut, swollen face, and turned his head away.

"Ah," she said, "you are stupid, stupid."

She smiled at his puzzled stare. She cupped her breasts
in her hands and said, "Because to me you are beautiful
now."

His mouth crushed her teeth against her lips. She uttered
a startled cry of pain and stifled it. He heard it and drew
back.

"No, no, querido," she gasped, and unbuttoning her gown
she bared her breasts and thrust them upwards to meet his
mouth. She made little whimpering cries of ecstasy and then
sat up panting and pressing her breasts against him, as she
pulled the gown over her head. She held him hard and
pressed her long thighs against him and ran her hands up
and down his back, kissing his throat, and she whispered,
crying with joy, "I thought it would be so bad, I am so
grateful, I am so grateful!"

In the half-dark he tasted her tears as they slid into his
mouth. He felt a surge of love and protection that he had
never felt before, and he pulled her head back with a hand
wrapped in her hair and kissed her throat and her breasts.
She sobbed with delight.

Outside, leaning near the shutters, Bearclaw turned to
Archie, and tugged his elbow. Archie's ear was close to the
shutters. He jerked his elbow violently out of Bearclaw's
grip and squeezed closer to the wall. He was breathing hard
and swallowing nervously. Once more Bearclaw touched his
elbow. Archie flung him off again, savagely. Bearclaw stared
at him a moment and silently walked away. When he got
back to the table where the others were still playing poker
and yawning someone asked where Archie was.

"If I tole you you wouldn't believe me," Bearclaw
said. "I heard they got men like that come to cathouses down
in Austin who don't do nothin' but just pay to look. An' I
never believed it. Till tonight. An' by God, we got a Fisher
is one, he oughtta be ashamed of hisself."

Chapter Twenty-One

Carson ripped open the letter postmarked "Isleta, Texas" as he stood in the post office. The postmaster, one of King Fisher's numerous remote relatives, was staring at him with what Carson had come to realize was the "Fisher look"—a blend of anger, hostility, hatred, and puzzlement. Carson stepped out in the street and held the letter up against the light. It did not look as if it had been secretly opened.

The letter began abruptly: "No use trying to explain. Just consider that I guessed wrong about you. What gave me the feeling I could trust you was that the cattle on the Valdes place were just as you had represented them—and maybe a little bit better. You're a hard man in a bargain but a fair one. You and I could make a lot of money working together. I know the border country very good. I got contacts everywhere and I can raise capital to finance pretty big operations. But I need someone I can trust to run things down in Mexico. I got my eye on a mining operation which ought to produce so fast it will make ranching look like chicken feed. If we get on I'll let you in on that. The reason why I'm writing to you is that you're on the way up. If you can't beat 'em, join 'em—that's my motto. In a couple of years you'll have a big spread. King Fisher is only good for a few more years and from what I can see his kin will run that ranch into the ground with one bad winter. I need a good man to funnel my cattle to. You have some good men in the Valdes boys. Come down and we'll talk. To show my good faith I am letting you in on a good thing: the general is finished. He is right here in Texas, camped down the Rio Grande about thirty miles. The Mex army climbed all over him like a mad tomcat over a sick pup. My army contact says the general can stay in the States, but he can't make speeches, and if he don't give up his guns and horses and mules and most of his burros the U. S. Army will come from San Antonio and arrest him and the whole army of his, and deport them across the river, where the Mex army is waiting. So he will have to sell the stuff. Which he doesn't know yet. And he'll sell, you can bet on that. He has about 900 horses, 500 carbines, not too much ammunition, 250 burros, and about 3500 cattle. You might have some trouble with the Cattlemen's Association inspectors as far as the cattle are concerned, but we can make some deal with the Mex army people to let the cattle across the river. Then we could trail them to Arizona and cross the river fast and get rid of them. I think the lot can be picked up for $50,000. No need to tell you what the profit would be on the cattle. I hear the Comanches are paying up to a hundred for carbines. The British are offering up to $75 for burros for the Zulu War. I'll let you in for half, when we clear this up we can move on to really big things. Bring a few men you can trust. The general's men are prowling around here sticking up ranches and if you come down with that kind of money you better be careful. Hoping to hear from you soon—the army will move against him in two weeks from above date. Keep this letter confidential, Very sincerely yours, D. Bond."

Carson put the envelope in his pocket. He walked into the barber shop and took a chair. As the barber covered his face with hot towels he leaned back, completely relaxed, and began to do some hard thinking.

If it was a straight offer he would make out very well. Was it a trap?

It didn't read like one—not with that reminder to bring a reliable escort with him. If he went down he would always travel with the Valdes men as a bodyguard. He would ship out the best cattle and the best horses. He would handle the carbine deal himself—this would be a delicate operation and he preferred to handle it alone rather than entrust it to Bond. It was the kind of deal which produced the fastest and largest profit, and in cash.

Perhaps, he thought, as he felt the warm steamy towels around his face, the carbines should go north immediately. Bond would handle the cattle. He would say good-by, shake hands with Bond, leave openly with the carbines and his bodyguard, and then it would be easy to slip back alone (or if he found a good hiding place for the guns) with the Valdes men, find the general, and kill him. With luck he would get Pablo also.

Then he would take the cash from this operation and ride into Sonora with Luisa. He would avoid coming near the border until everyone had calmed down. He would refuse Bond's further offers of partnership until that time.

The first thing necessary would be to telegraph Bond he would come. He would have to do this from another town. Then he had to find a buyer for his ranch. It would not do to arouse King Fisher's suspicions. He knew that he could not sell it from Sonora, through a land agent's office 1400 miles away in a town controlled by King Fisher.

The more he thought about it the more he liked it. Bond would perform, unknowingly, the important function of bringing him and the general together. And, as a result, Carson would make an excellent profit, eliminate the general, and become the owner of a vast hacienda bigger than King Fisher's ranch, and so far south that he need not trouble himself about King Fisher's desire to avenge himself. Or Bond's. Or the damn Fisher clan's.

Yes, he thought with a rush of satisfaction. Better to clear out of the damn country. He would always have to be careful about the Fishers—they would never forgive the death of the old watchman. Sooner or later he would be bushwhacked—maybe a shot would be fired from the sagebrush as he would ride out into the blazing sun from a dark canyon, maybe a shot would come in through a window at night as he would be sitting eating supper.

That was what would happen even with King Fisher's hard restraining hand on them. What would happen if that hand were removed? He would sweat it out every time he passed close to a thicket.

"How's that, Mr. Carson?"

He looked at the mirror absent-mindedly. "Fine, just fine," he said, nodding. He put on his jacket, paid the barber, and stepped into the street. He had to wire Bond and withdraw his account from the bank.

"Sure he didn't see yuh?"

"Sure, Mr. King Fisher," said the barber. It was next afternoon. The barber held onto a stirrup. His other hand held a razor. "His face was all covered up with hot towels, even his eyes."

"Sure he didn't hear yuh open the envelope? Or hear yuh readin' it?"

"Nope. There was some kids yellin' an' playin' outside an' a couple big teams was goin' by. I wouldn'ta looked at a man's private mail 'cept I saw the postmark said Isleta an' I know you got a big interests down there. Else," he added virtuously, "I wouldn'ta touched it."

"I'll take care of you," said King Fisher. He started to trot away. He stopped and trotted back. He whistled as the barber was about to re-enter his shop.

The barber came to him eagerly.

"Mister Wheat."

"Yes, Mr. King Fisher?" the barber said, happily expectant.

"Mister Wheat," said King Fisher softly, leaning down, "you are not to talk about that letter to anyone. Never. At no time. If you do, I'm gonna hear about it. If I hear about it, I'll be back to see yuh." He reached down, took the hand holding the razor, bent the palm inward, and lifted Wheat's paralyzed forearm until it was at the height of its owner's jugular. Then he moved the arm quickly from left to right.

"Unnerstan'?"

Mr. Wheat nodded nervously. King Fisher grinned down at him and trotted out of town.

"You really surprised me, Carson," King Fisher said, "wantin' to sell out."

Carson shrugged. "Can't work for you an' run a ranch at the same time," he said.

"Hire someone. Someone you can trust." He leaned forward out of his hammock and said, "Git yourself a light from my cigar."

Carson leaned forward and puffed. Their eyes met. Carson had the sudden feeling that King Fisher knew he was lying, but he dismissed this as the workings of a guilty mind. As King Fisher leaned back and stared at him in a friendly fashion Carson thought, with relief, that he was imagining things.

"Too hard to find anyone," he said. "And any money I plow into that ranch, into artesian wells, into windmills, into bob wire, blooded stock—that's all wasted unless I can be there steady. An' the taxes eat away at my bank account."

"It's hard to find a man you can trust," nodded King Fisher.

"So I figger sell it for a good price, put the money into safe bonds, like U.S. bonds, get a good safe int'rest rate, work for you for a few years, bank all that too, an' then I can start off clean."

"Fair 'nough. What're yuh askin'?"

"Stock, ranchhouse, corrals, as is—eighty-five thousand."

"That's a lot, Carson." King Fisher frowned.

"World couldn't beat it for a good summer range."

"That's true."

"And couldn't be beat neither for winters."

King Fisher nodded. Carson went on.

"Plenty of arroyos with willow an' cottonwood. Good shelter from the northers. Cool in summer. When it's snowin' cattle could find their way there easy. You could store fodder there. Horses could eat the cottonwood bark. When the snow melts I got plenty of clay tanks built up at the bottoms of the run-offs to catch the water an' hold it all summer. Rollin' country means cattle could climb some an' let the breeze up there blow away flies."

"You know your ranchin'. You'll be a big man someday."

"How long did it take you to get to know it?"

"I been at it thirty-one years, an' I learn somethin' new every day. You never get any diplomas in the cow business. An' I come here when there wasn't a fence or a railroad in the whole state of Texas.

"I'm glad you're gonna give yore full time to the King Fisher spread, Carson. Gimme four years of yore time an' you ain't gonna want yore own place. It's pretty excitin' runnin' a big place like this one. An' lately I get to thinkin' how pleasant it would be to unbuckle my gun belt an' throw it in the fire an' watch someone who uses his head more than just somethin to separate his chin from his scalp run it. An' ridin' round them big steers at night with the moon shinin' on their big horns is a sight to make a man's eyes pop. Think maybe you'll change yore mind 'bout goin' off on yore own. Eighty thousand."

"Eighty-four."

"Eighty-one."

They grinned.

"Eighty-two five," said Carson.

"Done."

They shook hands on it. "I'd like a week off," Carson said, casually.

"Sure."

"Want to go to San Antonio an' buy U.S. bonds."

"What about your gal?"

"I'm takin' her to San Antonio. She's gonna go on to Galveston by stage an' take a boat to Vera Cruz."

"Thought she wouldn't want to go back to Mexico."

"Thought so too. But I talked her into it."

"All right," said King Fisher, grinning and starting the hammock to swinging by shoving his boot at the floor. "I'll have the money tomorrow afternoon. An' if you had any sense, you'd marry that gal. Much too valuable to be floating 'round Texas." He laced his hands behind his back and watched Carson walk out.

"Eighty," said King Fisher. "Eighty-one. Eighty-one five. Eighty-two. An' eighty-two five."

Carson put the money into two big saddlebags.

"I'd feel better if you counted it," said King Fisher.

"I trust you," said Carson. He gave the bags to Sebastiano, who took them outside. Through the doorway King Fisher watched Sebastiano throw them over Carson's horse.

"Well, now," said King Fisher, lazily, "that's a real nice compliment. Mighty nice." Sebastiano's nephews, he noticed, had good horses and were well-armed. Two burros carried their food and bedding. Luisa sat waiting. King Fisher came outside with Carson. "Take care of yoreself," he said cheerfully. "Don' wanna lose a good man. *Adios, Señorita, vaya con Dios.*"

"*Y usted. Gracias.*"

"*Hasta la vista,* Carson."

"*Hasta la vista.*"

He watched them ride off.

Bearclaw came out and said, "You're crazy, aincha? Givin' him all that money! You know he's got another forty thousand on 'im too? Why woncha let us bushwhack him? We could ride ahead an' pick 'em off tomorrow at sundown. They gotta make camp in Arroyo Hondo. With Archie an' me an' ol' Dave it would be a cinch."

"No. An' ol' Dave sucks that bottle of bourbon like it's sugar titty."

"No one ever'd connect it with us. Then we'd ride south a couple days, cross the breaks of the Quitaque, an' come up north again. No one'd see us that way."

"No."

"Doncha hate to see all that Fisher money goin' away forever? I don't understand you, by God, I don't. You gettin' soft in the head thinkin' about that de Parral gal?"

King Fisher turned and stared at Bearclaw.

Bearclaw mumbled, "Sorry."

King Fisher grunted. Bearclaw went on, "Let us go down an' take care of it. We'll leave the gal alone. Don' worry about old Dave. He can shoot. He can ride. An' he can keep his mouth shut. An'—"

"You're a damn fool," King Fisher observed amicably. "An' I'll tell you why. I'm goin' down to Isleta myself. *I'm* gonna make the deal with the general to buy him out. For that I'm gonna need money. Why should I carry money down with me an' worry about bein' jumped for it all the way down there? Let Carson worry about it. He'll take good care of it with the Valdes boys with him. Damn good care, as good as I could take care myself. An' when he gets down there, guess who'll be there to greet him with both arms? Eh?"

Bearclaw's mouth opened in a wide grin of admiration. "We'll take the money off him with a polite thank you, mister."

Bearclaw said with enthusiasm, "*That's* the place to bushwhack!"

"But first we gotta go see Mr. Bond an' maybe spank 'im to show 'im there's some life in the old bastard still, eh? But I need him. So I'll spank 'im only a little bit. There's lots of good information in him. I might try to buy some good Mex mining property. Or even into some Mex railroads. An' when I'm down in Sonora he'll be mighty useful to do my border business for me. An' with someone up there I can trust runnin' the old KF—"

"You gonna *stay* in Sonora?"

"That de Parral gal made an offer to Carson. He don't look too interested to me. Or mebbe he is—but he won't be able to do nothin' about it. I'll come by, an' tip my hat, an' say, 'Beggin' your pardon, ma'am, but I hear tell you've got a general to be murdered in exchange for a hacienda.' An' she'll say, 'Why, yes, señor, that ees true.' An' I'll say, 'If you'll step this way, ma'am, I will make you a very dead general.' "

"But who's gonna run the KF?"

"You, Bearclaw."

"Holy Moses."

"But you gotta do as I say. Keep Archie in line. Smack 'im around if you have to. I'll come up twice a year to look around the ranch. You better keep yore nose clean, boy. Give some people a break an' they want the moon for a cow pasture.

"Now, when we get down to Isleta, we gotta take possession, very legal, 'cause the U.S. Army'll be snoopin' around, of all the general's horses an' burros an' carbines and get a signed receipt offen him. That's why we gotta handle Bond gentlelike. He'll arrange all that. We'll have to hand over Carson's cash to the general. We can take it back later, don't get your hackles up. That might take some doin'. He's no prairie flower, that one. He ain't gonna trust me at all, he ain't trustin' no one, he'll have his bodyguard everywhere he moves, day 'n night. Nobody's gonna trust nobody, matter of fact. I don't want anyone jumpin' the gun or shootin' off his mouth down there. We'll need some very careful shootin'. That reminds me, what's Archie doin'?"

"Tomcattin' around."

"Get 'im. Tell 'im I got a job for him he'll like. Tell 'im it's somethin' he's been achin' to do a long time. As long ago as the first time he ran across Mr. Carson sleepin' down in Mexico."

"He'll come a-runnin'," said Bearclaw.

Dave came out of the ranchhouse and walked unsteadily toward them. His walk was still energetic.

"That ole buzzard stewed again?" asked King Fisher, irritated. "He'll suck all the loose whisky in Isleta."

"He mought be old," said Bearclaw, "but he's a hard man with a gun."

They watched the unlettered, unclean old man with his savage tobacco-stained white mustaches waver towards them. He wore a filthy buckskin vest and a turnip watch he had once stolen in a train holdup. The watch had not worked for years; he always used to say that he would get it fixed some day and in the meantime the safest place for it was right where it was, across his belly at the end of that heavy gold chain.

"That soupstrainer of yourn looks like a dead snow-rabbit strapped under yore nose," said Bearclaw.

"Shet up, you danged fool," said Dave, in a high-pitched voice. "This hand has tanned that backside of yourn before an' it's itchin' to do it again, sheriff star or no, you heah?"

"Wanna go for a ride, granpop?"

"Nope."

"You wanna stay here an' be a practice post for the kids to drop a riata over?"

"Me an' the pet goose," said old Dave. "We don't mind. Better that than lissen to yore loose lips goin' flap-flap with no sense comin' out."

"When you gonna fix that damn watch you stole?"

"This am a wicked an' parvarse generation of vipers, young man," Dave said, holdin' on to the corral rail for support. "None of yore damn business."

"Granpop—"

"How come none o' you young bulls took out after that Mex gal? She got lips rosy as a perch's gills, stands sixteen an' a half hands high, prob'ly weighs a hunnerd twenty-six in her petticoat tail afore breakfast. An' her hair's as slick as this yere bottle an' long as a hoss' tail. I seen it comin' down her back when she was a-combin' it in the sun. Twenty years ago I woulda clumb all over this Carson feller for her. An' I ain't goin' down there to Isleta. The brush is so damn thick you can't stick a knife in it an' everythin' in the country has either got stickers on it or it's poisonous."

"But you're goin'," said King Fisher.

"No, I ain't. You ain't got no call to order me aroun', boy," he said savagely. "You take keer of us Fishers, you give us orders. You're settin' up this here Carson like a king himself, you kin go to hell."

"Dave, it's all different now," Bearclaw said soothingly.

"Shet up!"

"We're gonna take care of Carson now, it's all fixed."

"You? You gotta go around with somebody, kid, you ain't never alone, you or Archie. You go on the gun route, you gotta be by yourself. You gotta have someone always holdin' your hand. It's gonna take all of us to bushwhack him. I got no more guts either." He staggered back inside for another drink.

"He'll be all right when he's sobered up," said King Fisher. He put his palms on his thighs and leaned forward.

"If you or anybody touches that de Parral gal," he said softly, "or even looks at her crossways, I'll have the pleasure of watchin' a buzzard pull his guts out of his asshole. Pass the word. An' get ready. We're leavin' in an hour."

Chapter Twenty-Two

"Put away that star, you damn fool," said King Fisher. He leaned forward in his saddle and tapped on the big plate glass window that said "D. BOND RANCH PROPERTIES." Several Mexican vaqueros were lounging on the sidewalk gambling for ammunition with a greasy pack of cards.

Bond looked up from his desk. The day had been hot and he was gently waving a fan back and forth.

Dave Starr leaned back in his saddle and chuckled. "He looks like his head just been took off," he said. "Drained dryer'n a pint of liquor among forty men. I'm ridin' down the street for a drink."

"Don't get lost, you ol' fool!" said King Fisher.

Bond came out, still holding his fan. "Pleased to see you, King Fisher," he said. "Come in and sit a while."

King Fisher dismounted and tossed the reins to Archie.

"Hi, Bond," said Bearclaw. Bond nodded nervously.

"Pretty hot, ain't it?" asked Bond. He sat down and gave his fan to King Fisher. King Fisher sat on the edge of the desk and waved the fan gently back and forth. He said nothing. The sweat began to form on Bond's face. King Fisher watched it roll down. He waved the fan in Bond's direction.

"Looks like a Mex town," said King Fisher. He nodded toward the vaqueros sprawled on the boardwalks.

"Ain't no Rangers nearer'n El Paso," said Bond. "An' that's ninety miles. We got a sheriff but I got 'im elected, so he's no good for nothin' except doin' what I tell him to. He's out chasin' the town drunk, says the old cripple stole the Briggs' gal's pet lamb. Claims the Briggs gal cries herself to sleep every night. When he heard the general was pilin' 'cross the river towards Isleta he took out real fierce after that lamb-rustler. There's a couple companies of calvary, but they're up at Fort Duncan, fifty miles west. They got a couple patrols

139

ridin' around, but you never know where the hell they are, so they ain't any good. Nobody here's pickin' a fight with them vaqueros, they're plenty tough, and the town's crawlin' with 'em."

"Where's the Mex army that chased the general over to Isleta?"

"About ten miles the other side of the river; ten miles inside Mexico. They got patrols out day and night ridin' up and down the river on their side."

"How come they're so far back?"

"The Mex army's got orders to stay plenty far away from the border. Presidente Diaz is lookin' for U. S. money to invest in his railroads and his industry, so he don't want to risk no incidents with any U. S. citizens. You know how it is, some one'll see a Mex soldier pretty close to the river an' he'll take a pot shot at him, and a couple of his amigos will take across the river to get even. An' then there's the U. S. troops—maybe some hot-headed Mex officer will order his men to fire at them, and then they'll fire back, and then all hell will break loose. Even a real genuine Mex general might get excited, lookin' at a couple Rangers within carbine range, or maybe he might see a couple of the boys you see sittin' there gamblin' for cartridges, and he'd order a charge across the river. So old Diaz is no fool."

"So the general's runnin' the town?"

"You might say so."

"Ain't you ashamed?"

"No."

"You a Texan?"

Bond stared at his hands. His face flushed pink.

"Hot even for the valley," Bond went on. He wiped his face with a handkerchief.

"I ain't rode three hundred miles real hard to talk about the weather," King Fisher said.

Bond opened a cigar box and offered it. "Real Havana," he said proudly. King Fisher smelled one, nodded, and shoved a handful into his pocket. He took another handful and gave them to Archie. "I don't smoke," Archie said.

"I know damn well you don't smoke," said King Fisher, testily. "But I got no more room in my pocket." Archie sullenly shoved them in his pocket. Bond struck a match and held the flame in front of King Fisher. His hand trembled slightly. King Fisher smiled and struck a match himself. He held it beside Bond's match. King Fisher's hand was steady as a granite boulder.

"Clean livin', Bond. Try it. And another way I keep healthy—I trust myself. No one else."

"Don't blame you," said Bond. The match burned his fingers. He cursed and dropped it.

"A man ain't careful," went on King Fisher, "he can burn himself. Know what I mean?"

"Sure, sure."

"Mebbe you don't, Bond. I read the letter you wrote Mr. Carson." He began to unbuckle his gun belt. "Pity God didn't put fur on some people so's you could shoot 'em at sight." Bond stared, his mouth open. Archie moved close to the desk and put his hand on his gun butt.

"I'm gonna tan yore hide," said King Fisher, amiably, "jus' to prove I'm gonna be around a bit longer. Stand up."

"Take it easy, King Fisher. I don't blame you for gettin' steamed up. The letter is a fake."

"Take off yore gun belt, Bond."

"I'm tellin' you, the letter is a fake!"

King Fisher sighed. "Come on, Bond," he coaxed. "Take it off."

Behind him King Fisher heard someone walk into the office.

"Archie, throw that feller out," said King Fisher, carefully placing his cigars on the desk. "Come on, Bond," he went on, "I wanna show you what the old man can still do."

"For the last time," said Bond, "that letter was a fake!"

Archie said, "I ain't throwin' this feller out."

"Do what I say," said King Fisher.

"He ain't no feller," said Archie. "He looks like a general to me. He's got lots of men with 'im, too. You better turn around."

"Mr. Bond," said King Fisher, "you will excuse me. Only for a while, mind you."

He turned around. The general was leaning against the window with his arms folded. Outside, their faces pressed against the glass, were several of his men.

"That your private army?"

The general raised an assenting palm.

"Señor King Fisher."

"Well?"

"Bond an' me, we write the letter. A good letter, no?"

King Fisher turned to Bond and said, "Beg your pardon."

Bond glowered in silence. King Fisher turned back to the general.

"Like our business arrangement. It got complicated, but it straightened out all right. Sorry you had to come over this side." He buckled on his belt again. Bond sank back in his chair with a sigh of relief.

The general shrugged. "War is like ranching, there are good years and bad years, no? This is a bad year."

"Yeah," said King Fisher, amused.

"I want to see this Carson again. Mr. Bond, too. We write a good letter, we wait. Also Sebastiano Valdes I don' like, I take care of him, too. We been waitin' on the road, one week now, day an' night we watch. We don' see him. Mebbe you see?"

"No. We rode so's we wouldn't catch up with him. We rode way east. We wouldn'ta seen them. We figgered we'd catch them around here."

"Three big spiders," said the general, "waitin' for some little flies with money."

"Thought I'd jus' remind you, gennelmen," said King Fisher, "that's my money the flies'll be carryin'. I don' want no arguments 'bout that."

"Your money?" grinned the general.

"I bought his ranch. He's got that money with him. An' then he's got the money he cleared for himself on our little deal."

"That's my money," said the general.

"A lot of it is mine," said Bond. "I didn't want to buy those carbines at the price he set on them."

"I figger it's all my money," King Fisher said heavily.

The general held out his hands, palms up. "That money," he said, "it belongs to the first one that gets it, no?"

"I don't like your attitude," said King Fisher. "If we're gonna fight over whose money it is before we ever see Carson we ain't ever gonna be friends, let alone run across him. So let's put it this way. If you get it first, it's yours. If we get it first, it's ours. If we both get it together, half and half."

"Bueno, bueno!"

Bond opened a drawer and set a bottle of bourbon on the table. He poured out two glasses. King Fisher asked him why not three. "You know I don't drink," said Bond. King

Fisher and the general drank theirs, while Bond asked, "What's your next step?"

"He's comin' in, jus' how we don't know. He's smarter than us. He thinks he is, he don't know he's walkin' into our bear trap. But how he's comin' we don't know. We'll just have to sit here, with men prowlin' around the country to scout for him. I'll think of some way to suck him in."

The general began to chuckle. He filled up his glass again and began to shake with laughter.

"What's funny?" asked King Fisher.

"Don' worry," said the general. "I fix it so Carson come in to Isleta fast, fast! We sit here an' be cool an' make him come to us, you see!"

Chapter Twenty-Three

Sebastiano and Carson swam the river first, holding their carbines high in the air to keep them dry. When they had come ashore in Texas Sebastiano turned to Carson and, placing his gnarled brown hand on Carson's arm, said, "Ay, patrón, we made it!"

He turned and waved the others across. When they had, in turn, swum the river from Mexico, they rode on, carbines across their saddle horns. Up to now they knew that their approach through Mexico had let them move unseen. But now Isleta was only a few miles away. They might run into the general any second.

Old Sebastiano became jittery with excitement. He had never been away so long before from his wife, and unable to control himself any longer, he let out several shrill coyote yelps and he and his nephews raced ahead.

They had had no fears about leaving her alone. Sebastiano was sure that the general and his forces would melt southward, in groups of two or three ordinary looking vaqueros, and reform again where they had originated, in Sonora. Very seldom did Indians pass through the area of the little ranchito, and for ordinary problems she could easily handle anything that might come up with her Winchester: Sebastiano had taught her to shoot well, and he was proud of her.

Carson turned and looked at Luisa. She was riding with her head down. He could not see her face, but he instinctively knew that she was thinking that if she were ever to return home to Sonora there would be no such delight. He was moved by her suppressed grief. His own home, ever since he could remember, was wherever he happened to roll up for the night in his blanket, his only hearth a tiny

fire of buffalo chips burning at his feet. The three galloping
men disappeared ahead at a bend in the road.

When Carson and Luisa rode into the yard they saw the
three Mexicans standing at their horses' heads, waist deep
in the weeds and wildflowers. Horses had pawed and trampled the corn, crushing twelve little chickens to death. A log
had been placed between the roof of the adobe and the fork
of a cottonwood. Senora Valdes and her two young grandsons
hung from it. Two half-burned wagons stood in the corral,
the fence of which was burning. In the corral lay the carcass of a burro. Two pots and a kettle hung from the low
fire-seared branches of a little tree near the house, while
underneath a few cackling chickens were huddled together.

Underneath the body of Senora Valdes two shovels had been
tossed. It was a message, Carson realized, that said, as
plainly as if it had been written, that Sebastiano had been
saved the trouble of looking for them.

Carson hoped that Sebastiano would not see what he had
just noticed: her murderers had ripped off her gold earrings
through her ear lobes. But when the graves had been dug
and the time come to wrap her in a sheet Sebastiano saw.

As soon as the last shovelful of dirt had been thrown
Sebastiano mounted, rammed his spurs hard, and sawed his
horse's head toward Isleta. Never before had the old man
treated his horse so savagely.

Carson reached quickly and grabbed the reins. Sebastiano,
white-faced, tried to pull the reins from Carson's grip.

"Adonde vas?" shouted Carson, above the frightened and
agonized whinnying of the horse, which was being spurred
by his rider while at the same time Carson had pulled its
head sharply around to his withers. The galled, puzzled,
tortured horse thrashed in a circle to his left while Sebastiano, beginning to weep with frustrated rage, tried to jerk
the reins out of a grip that was stronger than any force he
could muster.

"Deje-me, deje-me!" Sebastiano pleaded, "Let me go,
let me go!"

Carson shook his head.

"Por favor!"

"No, no," said Carson, "he wants you to ride into ambush,
we will talk and make a plan. *Hombre,* listen!"

"I know these sons of whores! They don't wait for days in
ambush! They're in town drinking and whoring, let me go!"

"He's right!" said the older of the two boys, swallowing his tears. He reached out and tried to pull his uncle's reins out of Carson's grip.

Carson tried to soothe the old man, who suddenly pulled his Colt and cocked it.

"Patrón! Oiga me! Por el amor de Dios!"

Carson looked at the cocked trigger and the plunging horse. He knew with absolute sureness that if he did not let go, the old man, with the greatest of regret, would kill him. He let go.

The three men galloped towards Isleta.

Luisa came alongside and stared at them.

Then she turned to Carson.

"Oye, Tejano," she said. Her voice was icy.

"What?"

"Are you going?"

"I'm not crazy."

"Listen. The spider has made a web to catch the fly." She pointed to the grave. "And he put honey everywhere, no?"

"Well?"

"So you think you are clever if you don't walk in?"

"Go on."

"But if the fly wants the spider just as much as the spider wants the fly, what's the best way to find the spider quickly?"

"Shake the web with both hands. But I want to live a little longer than Sebastiano does."

"Then you stay here and wait till we come back and tell you what happened in Isleta. *Adios, querido.*" She began riding towards Isleta.

"Goddammit!" said Carson. He rode after her. He grabbed her reins and pulled her horse to a halt. She put her hand on her gun butt.

"Take your hand off," she said softly.

"All you goddam Mexicans!" said Carson, with admiration and exasperation. He took his hand off the reins. She resumed her course.

"You wait here," Carson said. *"I'll* tell you what happened."

"And suppose the general sends someone here while you're in Isleta? The safest place is right inside the web."

"Christ Almighty! Stop talkin' in proverbs or whatever the hell it is!"

"I want very much to see the general. And Pablito. Oh, I

want to see Pablito very much, please, just once more before
we ride across the river and never come back to Texas."

Once more he reined in, on the verge of forcing her back.

"*No, querido,*" she said. "I come."

He hesitated, looking at the set, lovely mouth, aware of
her icy, yet savage calm.

"And then," she said, "then I will sleep without bad
dreams. So kiss me."

He bent over. She kissed him so fiercely that their teeth
grated together.

"And you promise, afterwards we ride across the river?"

"Sure."

"On the honor of your mother?"

"*Palabra de honor,*" said Carson, and he slapped her horse
on the croup as he dug his spurs into his horse's flanks.

Chapter Twenty-Four

"You got a map of Isleta somewheres?" King Fisher asked. Bond nodded. He pulled down a huge wall map.

"Where are we?"

Bond pointed.

"All right," said King Fisher. "Where's old Valdes' place?"

"Out along this road."

"So they'd come along this road here, right?" said King Fisher softly. "An' turn down this street where we are now?" Bond nodded.

King Fisher went on, still speaking softly. "An' come down and put their paws right into the middle of our delicate bear trap and BANG!" He clapped his two huge hands together as hard as he could and roared as Bond nervously jumped. "All right. Any way they kin ride out of town?"

Bond stared at the map.

"There's a little alley up the street a little," he said. "Aside from that they got to ride all the way back to this fork where they came into town. Or they can ride two hundred yards more and then cut into the chaparral."

"So all we have to do," said King Fisher, "is let them get right next to us, right next to this here office of yours—and then plug both ends of the bottle. A couple men to cover the alley."

"That—that's it."

"You a little nervous?"

"A little. I tell you frankly, gunfightin' ain't in my line."

"This ain't gunfightin'," King Fisher said contemptuously. "This is shootin' fish in a barrel. No call to get excited. General, you'll set about six, seven men here—" King Fisher noticed but disregarded the narrowing of the general's eyes, "—right where the road forks comin' from the Valdes place. Then you—"

The general lifted a finger and slowly wagged it back and forth as he leaned toward the street and listened. He leaned backwards in his chair and grinned and pointed toward the street.

Pablo galloped up, slid off his panting horse, and jangled into Bond's office.

"*Que pasó?*" demanded the general. Pablo talked into the general's ear, grinning at Archie.

"*Ay, bueno!*" said the general, clapping Pablo on the back, and turning to King Fisher he said, "The flies are coming!"

"Haylo," Pablo said to Archie, and added very slowly and distinctly, "How-do-you-do?" He had gotten over his habit of covering his mouth when he spoke.

"Pablo speak English very good," said the general.

"*Si*, good!"

Old Dave walked into the office. He sank into a chair with a groan of pleasure, saw the bottle of bourbon, heaved himself up again, took the bottle, sat down with it and a glass, and poured himself a full glass.

"We'll have to spot our men around," said King Fisher. "I got five men."

"Looks more like four," said Bond, staring at old Dave's adam's apple as he gulped down the whisky.

"He can hold his own, don't worry," said King Fisher. "Bond, how many men you got?"

Bond said, pale, "Three."

"Plenty," said the general, "I got plenty."

"How many?"

The general looked at him. "*Tejano*," he said softly, "I tell you not to worry. I got plenty."

"Don't call me *Tejano*, an' don't tell me not to worry. Don't tell me nothin'. I don't want no trouble with you before we finish with Carson. How many carbines you got?"

The general said nothing. He sat on the desk and put his palms on his greasy charro pants, elbows out. He rubbed his palms up and down slowly. King Fisher knew he was drying his palms in case he had to make a fast move to draw. Pablo sprawled back against the window sill, pushing a huge gold earring on one finger after the other. The left hand was holding the earring, the right hand was still, and placed against his thigh, close to his gun butt.

"You like to give orders, no?" asked the general.

"In Mexico yo're a general," said King Fisher, lifting

his eyebrows and staring at Pablo. Archie understood and turned casually and faced Pablo, his right hand hooked in his belt.

"Here I'm a general," King Fisher went on. "If you don't like it there's the Rio Grande. How many guns you got here?"

"I tell you, what you do?"

"What'll I do? Crissake, I'm a spy. I'll write letters to Mexico City—what the hell you think I want to know for? You're gettin' hysterical as a schoolgirl."

The general put his hand on his gun butt, but King Fisher had his on his inlaid butt first. Dave chuckled and hugged himself with pleasure.

"Gentlemen, gentlemen!" said Bond, in agony.

"Evvabuddy kill evvabuddy else in this yere office," said Dave, "it'll make the funniest damn story. Evvabuddy in Texas split their sides laughin' at us Fishers. Now cut it out, god-dammit!" he roared, smashing his fist on the cigar box. "You're like a bunch of kids, you-all need a good kick in the ass!"

"You ruined my Havanas, you old fart!" shouted Bond, as he cowered against the wall.

Dave went for his gun. The general roared with laughter, and King Fisher hooked his right arm into Dave's bent right arm as the old man went for his Colt. Dave gave up in disgust. "You bunch o' sheep guts!" he shouted, and headed for the door.

"Where you goin'?" demanded Bearclaw, blocking him.

"I'm headin' for a drink straightern' an Indian goin' to shit," said Dave. "Now git outta my way."

"Looky here," Bearclaw began.

"I said git." Dave's hand settled on his gun butt.

"Oh, for Crissakes," said Archie, "let him get a drink. He's gettin' real mean."

"He ain't gonna sweeten up with rotgut, Archie."

"Let 'im go, let 'im go," said King Fisher, disgusted. Bearclaw reluctantly stepped aside.

"That's one less man we got," said Bond.

"The odds are still pretty good," said King Fisher. A horse's hooves drummed suddenly down the dust-filled street. A vaquero leaned and shouted through the door, *"Mi general!"*

The general walked quickly to the door.

"Alla vienen quatro hombres, una mujer, Doña de Parral!"

The general motioned the man to take up a position across the street. The man dismounted, slapped the horse on the hip, and as the horse trotted toward his stable, the man ran across the street and posted himself in an alley.

"There goes my plan, goddammit!" King Fisher said. "Scatter and use your common sense. If you got any, which I doubt." The men scattered. Some ran across the street, some clattered upstairs. Bond went on his knees behind the desk.

"What the hell you gonna do?" demanded King Fisher. "Pray?"

Bond opened his desk drawer and pulled out a Colt. "I want some protection, that's all." He closed the drawer. "The desk is made of oak, and here's where I'm gonna stay."

"Score's about fifteen to five, what the hell you afraid of? And one of the five's a woman." He laughed. "Come to think of it, ol' Dave did say we was a bunch of sheep guts."

"What the hell you talkin' about?" said the nervous and excited Bond. "They in sight yet?"

King Fisher walked calmly to the door and looked up the street. "Not yet," he said, and added immediately, "Yeah. There they come. And there's our Mr. Carson, right out front." He looked at the men stationed everywhere where there was good shelter.

"You know, Bond," he said casually, not looking at the man, "I never bushwhacked no one. Speakin' as a Fisher I just mought be ashamed of myself in five minutes." He looked critically at Archie, who was smiling to himself and moving his lips soundlessly. As King Fisher watched, Archie kissed a cartridge and levered it into the firing chamber. Bond jumped at the sudden sharp click.

"Where they now?" asked Bond.

"A couple hundred yards to go, Bond. You'll know better when you hear the firin' start.

"Oye, hombres!" called the general sharply from the roof. Three of his men looked up. He told them to sit on the sidewalk and go on with their gambling.

"Oye, King Fisher," the general called softly.

"What you want?"

"The mice are here for the cheese," the general went on. "No tricks with the money, *comprende?*"

When they were fifty feet from Bond's office the general yelled, *"Tiran!"*

Luisa's horse shuddered and staggered. The three men who had been told to gamble plunged wildly into the office and began to fire. Carson made a grab for the bridle of Luisa's horse but the horse fell dead, pinning her underneath. One of Valdes' nephews fell dead with three bullets in his back. His horse trotted off, dragging the dead man by a spur still jammed in the stirrup. One of the Mexicans who had plunged into the office from the street raced out again, pulled the dead man's carbine from his dead grip, and as he triumphantly waved it aloft, Carson shot him in the back. He fell, writhing.

King Fisher heard the general clattering down the stairs. Sebastiano had been hit in the lower jaw. Half of it had been carried away. The bullet went ranging upwards and through his brain, tearing out the top of his skull. It made an exit hole as big around as a silver dollar. He lay on his back a few feet from Luisa's horse. He was alive but unconscious.

Carson had flung himself from his horse, and together with Ricardo Valdes had plunged into a chile parlor. The woman cook was cringing in a corner next to the stove and screaming. Carson ran behind the counter and grabbed her arm. She pulled back, screaming louder than ever. He jerked hard and she fell flat on the floor. She closed her eyes and continued screaming.

"Shut up and don't move," said Carson. Holes appeared in the windows, in the counter. A ketchup bottle exploded just above him. The woman was showered with ketchup and broken glass. She opened her eyes, saw the ketchup and screamed again.

"Don't move!" Carson called out to Luisa. She understood and lay still. "Ricardo," said Carson, "someone's up in that second story window, see if you can—"

"Patrón," Ricardo said, apologetically.

Carson turned. Ricardo's right shoulder blade had been broken by a shot. Blood dripped out of his sleeve. Carson ripped a dish towel for a sling and shoved in another to stop the blood. Volley after ragged volley poured into the chile parlor. The woman's screams had settled down into a shrill monotone. Six inches above the two men, the counter splintered as the bullets smashed through. Occasionally some white powdery dust drifted down on them as a bullet dislodged some of the dried mud in the adobe wall.

King Fisher watched. He had not fired once.

Pablo watched the dying Sebastiano pull up his right leg, and kick it erratically like a frog, as the blood oozed from his mouth. His eyes were wide open but he was unconscious.

"Oye, Carson, Valdes wants to die but he can't die nohow!"

Pablo began crawling in the dust towards Luisa and her dead horse. Her carbine had been knocked out of her hands by her fall and lay just out of reach. As she saw Pablo crawling close she tried desperately to reach the carbine. She could not reach that far. Pablo reached the carbine and pushed it behind him. Her fingers clawed the dust in rage. He was only three feet from her. He pulled his Colt. Carson got in a snap shot which smashed the Colt's cylinder. Pablo shook his tingling hand and grinned, pressing flat. He reached out and grabbed one of her braids.

"Buenas tardes, Señorita," he said, and jerked her head till it was wrenched back violently against her right shoulder. She thrashed about, trying to free herself. Her hand clawed at the ground, and suddenly she picked up a handful of dust and threw it in his face. He recoiled, sneezing and coughing, his one eye temporarily blinded. He rubbed his closed eye and gasped, "Espere poquito, vamos a ver momentito," and he still held on to her braid.

A Colt with its butt studded with tiny silver playing cards skidded to a halt against her arm. She grabbed it and cocked it. Pablo shook his head once more, pulled his knife, and opened his tearing eye.

He lifted his knife and she fired.

The heavy bullet knocked him to one side. He got to his knees and looked down. The bullet had gone through his chest. He lifted the knife again and she fired three times, sobbing and cursing with each shot. He was knocked to his back by the impact. Once more he got to his knees and crawled towards her. She fired twice and missed. Pablo grinned, his left hand holding his chest. He lifted the knife high and plunged downwards as hard as he could. At the last possible moment she twisted sidewards and the knife went three inches into the dirt as he died.

King Fisher threw away his cigar. "Goddammit," he said, "and I had it all figgered out so nice." He walked into the street with the carbine under his arm. The firing slowed and then stopped as the puzzled men watched him.

He walked through the street to her horse. She stared upwards at him as she covered him with her Colt. "I kin count, Señorita," he said, looking down at her. "You've done fired it six times." He put down his carbine, put his shoulder to the dead horse, and shoved. The carcass rose and she slid out. "Your leg broken?" he asked. She shook her head.

He picked up the carbine and pulled out Sebastiano's Colt from its holster. He lifted the old man's right eyelid and then let it drop. He took her arm and walked towards the restaurant. Carson watched him come and raised his Winchester as they came in.

"What am I supposed to do?" he asked. "Surrender? You're covered, King Fisher."

"Put it down, boy," said King Fisher. He tossed the Colt to Carson, who caught it, surprised. "Git down flat," he told Luisa, and he walked behind the counter and lay down.

Carson stared at him, puzzled.

"You come to talk?" he demanded.

"Nope. Nothin' personal. Just evenin' out the odds."

"Why?"

"Jus' say it's more fun thataway. Can't you make the old slut shut up?"

"No," said Carson.

King Fisher grinned and jerked his head. "They can't figger out what's happenin' yet," he said. "They'll figger it out soon. What's the matter, boy?"

"I can't figger you out."

"Always be one step ahead of the crowd. Figger out what the smartest one of your enemy figgers you'll do next—an' then go ahead one more step."

"What advantage you got comin' here? Now you got everybody out there mad at you."

"Just say it was too easy with me out there. I ain't had so much fun in years as I figger to have with you mighty soon. Now you set back an' relax while my relatives start hollerin'."

"Still can't figger you."

"Always liked a man who took big chances. Now I'm takin' 'em. I feel fine. Now you jus' pile up yore cartridges and let's get ready."

Archie called from behind his pillar, "Hey, Bearclaw!"

"Yeah?"

"You see the son-of-a-bitch skip his Colt along to that gal?"

"I seen him, he's gone crazy. What the hell's he doin' there now?"

"I thought he went in to powwow an' they're keepin' him in there till they make their getaway."

"What the hell did he toss her the Colt for then?"

"To show he wanted to be friends. Jeez, I don't unnerstan'—hey, King Fisher, you all right?"

King Fisher grinned as he lay on his back.

"Yeah, I'm fine!" he bellowed.

"They got a gun in his back," said Bearclaw.

"Lissen, Bearclaw," said Archie, "if he gets killed—if he gets killed accidental—"

"Yeah, I know, they'll kill 'im if we don't let 'em get away."

Archie looked at him contemptuously.

"If he gets kilt," he said coldly, "then we inherit."

"Gets kilt?"

Archie said nothing.

"Jeez," Bearclaw breathed, comprehending at last. "Accidental."

"Yeah. Real accidental, you fat son-of-a-bitch."

"You're the boy who does the fine shootin'. You better do the best accidental shootin' of your life, kid."

"You mean shoot my uncle?" Archie said dryly.

"I'm shocked, kid."

"Don't be shocked, Bearclaw."

"Just make that shot that'll get us a million an' a half acres, eleven thousand head, fifteen artesian wells, three hundred an' fifty miles of bob wire, an' we'll have the governor of Texas lickin' our hands and rollin' over on his back to have his belly scratched every time we go down to Austin to give him his orders. Belly down there like an' old coon, Archie, an' get to work.

"An' the next shot is for Carson, that's the one I been waitin' for, Bearclaw."

King Fisher said thoughtfully, "You know about Archie an' his shootin'."

"Yep."

"Gimme yore hat."

King Fisher took it and pushed it above the counter edge. Archie fired and blew the lamp chimney a foot away from it to bits.

"He ain't strikin' an empty hook, that boy ain't. That's his way of tellin' us to go to hell. We gotta suck that boy out. He's too smart for the empty hat trick. He needs live bait." He turned and called to Luisa for his inlaid Colt. She slid it along the floor. He reloaded it.

"O.K.," he said. "Git ready." Carson crouched, ready to stand up and fire.

King Fisher took a deep breath and poked the Colt around the edge of the counter. Archie's eyes widened as he recognized King Fisher's gold wedding band: he fired instantly. Carson stood up and fired at him as Archie was ejecting the shell. Archie worked the lever so fast that when the bullet struck him he fired again. But the impact of the slug in his stomach made the shot go wild. He lurched sidewards from behind the pillar.

He walked very slowly along the sidewalk. He sat down on it. Then he got up and staggered a few paces and leaned against a wall. He held on to the window sill for a few seconds, his back to the street. Then he fell backwards, dead.

"A fair exchange," said King Fisher. He held up his right hand: the forefinger had been shot off. He wrapped a dish-towel around it.

The general had commandeered a wagon and built a barricade on it out of full sacks of corn. Several men were in it, their carbine barrels poking out at the ready. The wagon rattled by, the man firing at full volume. From their superior height they could easily rake the restaurant. One bullet creased the cook's arm. She screamed, and then made no sound.

The wagon turned around and started to make a second pass. Carson stood up while King Fisher fired at Bearclaw and the others across the street to make them keep their heads down. As the wagon neared, Carson coolly shot the horses. They went down, squealing and thrashing. One by one he shot the men. After the third, the rest broke and ran for cover. King Fisher ran to the door and pegged a shot after them.

A bullet seared his face. Across the street Bearclaw frantically worked his lever for his next shot.

King Fisher shot first. Bearclaw screamed like a rabbit and clutching his throat, fell to his knees, and choking, fell face downwards into the dust, which absorbed his arterial blood as fast as his heart pumped it out of his artery.

The general and Carson and King Fisher fired together. The general, who had run from the wagon and had by now gained the roof across the street, looked surprised and irritated. He straightened up from his half-crouch. He shook his head slowly and looked at his chest, where two red blotches were beginning to widen outwards. He looked puzzled, as if a complicated riddle in a difficult language had just been asked of him. He stared at King Fisher, and started to cross himself. Before he could finish, his shattered heart stopped. He fell backwards, but one leg slipped over the roof edge and hung there, swinging slowly back and forth, the bent silver pesos alternately flashing and deadening, flashing and deadening as the oscillations of the general's dead leg caught the late afternoon sun.

King Fisher had felt a dull thud in his left shoulder blade and a sharp pain near his heart. At first he thought Carson had hit him accidentally with his carbine barrel as he whipped the Winchester around to face the general on the roof, but not until he felt blood trickling down his back did he realize that he had been hit. It seemed to him that his backbone turned to pulp. He closed up like a concertina; there was no pain, only a cool interest in what was happening to him. He felt his knees giving way under him. The startled expression, followed by concern, that appeared on Carson's face amused him. Then his head dropped on his chest and he fell. He felt drowsy and very relaxed. He opened his eyes and stared up at the filthy ceiling.

Carson and Luisa were staring down at him. From the other end of town there came the regular clop-clop of a cavalry patrol entering Isleta. Carson stood up, warily. Everyone was disappearing down the alleys. A Mexican took old Dave's horse and calmly rode off with it.

King Fisher thought, "I'm out of luck today." Aloud he said, "We both got 'im. Even with my bum hand I take half the credit." He was amused once more by Carson's puzzled look. Carson bent down and said, "I can't hear you."

Then King Fisher knew he was going to die.

"All right," he shouted, "you better get out fast." From

Carson's expression he knew that the man could barely hear him. King Fisher went on. "Too many people'll start askin' questions."

"King Fisher—"

"Lemme finish," King Fisher said impatiently, "hard to hear you. Not much time. You hit the river runnin'. You done it before. Take my Colt an' give it to yore first son to teeth on. You hear? Take it, goddammit, while I can still see!"

Carson took it.

"Carson, you 'n me shoulda been Comanches a hunnerd years ago. If the buffalo would come back tomorrow I wouldn't be slow sheddin' to a breechclout an' I'd trade the whole KF shebang for a buffalo hoss and a lance. But look at my relatives, they'll piss it away in booze joints an' fam'ly squabbles. I wanted you to get it some day, you hard-luck bastard, but you were too smart for yoreself an' too smart for me. Adios, my big corrals, my brand, who the hell'll remember them in five years? Not a goddam person, not a goddam person—'cept you, Carson, Carson—" King Fisher suddenly realized that Carson had not understood a single word, something had been wrong with his voice, and in the three seconds of life left to him King Fisher heard Luisa say, "*Adios, Tejano.*"

He touched his inlaid gun butt for the last time and his head fell forward.

Chapter Twenty-Five

Bond cautiously lifted his head as Carson and Ricardo and Luisa galloped down the street. He walked out into the street and carefully he looked into the restaurant where the woman cook was still whimpering in a shrill monotone as she stared at the wreckage.

"Shut up!" said Bond.

Out in the street two cavalry officers were staring down at the bodies of Pablo and old Valdes. Four troopers on the roof were lowering the body of the general. Someone had already covered Archie and Bearclaw.

He went into the saloon. The bartender was taking down the shutters, which he had placed over the windows at the first sign of trouble.

Sitting alone at the dark bar was old Dave. "Where's my hoss?" demanded the old man, his voice slurred and high-pitched.

"Dunno," said Bond, still shaken.

"Don't tell me some greasy stinkin' Comanche took 'em! They like hosses better'n beef."

Bond watched a cavalry squad come to a halt and survey the dead horses still in the wagon traces.

"The dirty buggers ate my own saddle hoss oncet," said the thin voice in the rear of the saloon. "A crackerjack! While there was plenty of cattle around."

Dave got up and staggered along the bar. "You seen anythin' of my hoss?" he demanded of the bartender.

"No, old man, I hain't seen your hoss, I hain't seen 'im, but don't you cry about it. You'll find your hoss."

"I ain't cryin'! Dad blame you, I ain't cryin'. It's my natural tone of voice. Kick the stuffin' out of you, you goddam son-of-a-bitch!"

"I ain't fightin' with you, grandpop," said the bartender.

Dave clung to the bar with both hands in speechless fury.

"Gimme a double shot," said Bond.

"You?" said the bartender, surprised. "You don't drink."

"I do now. Gimme it!"

He gulped it down and turned to look at Dave.

"For crissake," he whispered to himself in awe.

"Whatsamatter, Mr. Bond, you all right?"

"For crissake," Bond repeated. "Look who owns the King Fisher ranch."

Dave stumbled out into the sun. "Kill the son-of-a-bitch who stole my hoss," he said, "I'll kill 'im! I'll roast 'im over a slow fire! Arm by arm! Leg by leg!" He stumbled and fell into the bloody dust of the street. "That hoss was a cracker-jack," he mumbled. "A crackerjack." He placed his face on the street and passed out.

"Gimme another double," said Bond.